THE
Sea Wolf's
Mate

THE HIDEAWAY COVE SERIES

The Griffin's Mate
The Sea Wolf's Mate
The Lightning Dragon's Mate

All the books in the series are standalone romances. Each focuses on a new couple, with no cliffhangers. They can be read in any order, but characters from previous books reappear in later ones, so reading in order is recommended for maximum enjoyment.

THE

Sea Wolf's Mate

ZOE CHANT

CHAPTER ONE
Jacqueline

"I'm sorry, you have the wrong number. Yes—no, I realize you dialed the number listed for the pizza parlor, but something's wrong with the interchange and I'm afraid… This is the sheriff's office, ma'am, I'm afraid I really can't take your pizza order."

Jacqueline rubbed her forehead as the caller let her know just how unacceptable that was. *This is what I get for taking the evening shift,* she thought. *That storm must have seriously messed with the phone lines. I knew I shouldn't have trusted the boss when he said it was all sorted…*

She bit back a sigh, careful not to let even a hiss of breath escape. The last thing she wanted was the woman on the other end of the line thinking she was sighing at *her*. Even if it was kind of the truth.

If the pizza-woman had been the first wrong number to call her today, that would be one thing. But no. The storm a few days back had come up from Hideaway Cove to the south, and like all bad weather that came from that direction, it had left havoc in its wake. Not only broken shutters and saltwater-whipped gardens, but electrical mix-ups. Computers went haywire, lights flickered… and phone lines got crossed.

The sheriff's office landline had somehow become mixed up with that of a pizza joint on the other end of town—and an auto shop, and the local kindergarten, and what felt like half the businesses within ten miles—and as if that wasn't enough, the connection was bad.

At least, Jacqueline assumed it was the bad connection that was making this caller squawk like a seagull descending on a garbage bin.

She rubbed her forehead, waiting for the woman's rant to come to an end.

"I—oh. You'd like to make a formal complaint? About me not providing you with an appropriate level of service? Well, you go right ahead, ma'am. We have a contact form on our website, or… you'd like me to type it out for you? Of course. That will be no problem *at all.*"

Jacqueline gritted her teeth as the woman on the other end of the line dictated a list of Jacqueline's many sins. Including not taking her damned pizza order. *Why don't you blame me for the weather, as well?*

"Thank you, ma'am, I'll make sure the sheriff receives this when he's next in. Excuse me?" Jacqueline blinked. "Well, he's…"

At the Spring Fling, celebrating the fact that winter's finally over. With the rest of the office, and most of the town… and my ex.

Jacqueline swallowed. "…He's out on another call at the moment, ma'am. But I'll put your note on his desk for his priority attention."

There was a dangerous silence at the other end of the phone. Jacqueline thought the woman was rallying her strength for another attack—and then the other phone clattered against something, and the noise of excited shouts clamored down the line. Jacqueline closed her eyes. *A teenagers' party. Something the town put on to keep them out of trouble while everyone's at the Spring Fling getting respectably tipsy… and this woman's stuck babysitting. No wonder she's annoyed.*

"Ma'am—"

"Forget about it. My neighbor has brought over snacks. No thanks to *you.*"

Jacqueline's breath caught in her throat as the woman slammed the phone down. Pinching the bridge of her nose, she set down her own receiver. Gently.

It doesn't matter how good it would feel to slam it down. You know Reg would take any breakages out of your pay.

And she couldn't afford that. She was *done.* All the scrimping and saving, all the extra hours and odd jobs and humiliation—she just had to wait for her final check to clear, and it would all be over. She'd have finally paid down her home loan.

She'd be free. Free to reclaim her life. Leave this crushingly small town and do all the things that had passed her by.

And no way was her first home-loan-free paycheck going to go towards replacing broken office equipment. She was going to cut loose. Stay out late at clubs, wear short skirts and too much make-up, all the fun things she'd spent the last decade and a half missing out on. No ball and chain, no mortgage, no responsibilities—

She flung herself back in her chair and spun around. When she stopped, she was looking straight at the oversized, framed family photograph that took pride of place on her boss' desk.

Five pairs of eyes stared back at her. Reg, his wife Susie, and their three beautiful children.

A lump formed in her throat. She looked down, but all that did was draw attention to her outfit. She'd fretted over it all week, because the Spring Fling was going to be *it* for her. The mortgage was the last remnant of her old married life she'd been dragging behind her and now it was finally meant to be time for her fresh start.

She was wearing a bra that the shop assistant had promised would give her "like, amazing self esteem", a silky dress that shimmered when she walked—heck, she was even wearing *heels*…

And then Reg had sauntered in just as she was putting the finishing touches on her make-up and said *Oh, by the way, you know Deirdre can't do the evening shift tonight because of her thing on the weekend, and I was wondering* and he'd hmm'd and haww'd and gone on about *and it's Jonesy's first Spring Fling since he made deputy and you know his Ma's going to be so proud* and *Now young Marsha, it would just be a shame for her to miss out, what with her not making it to her prom last year* and he'd made it the whole way around the office twice before getting to the meat of the matter:

Jacqueline's ex-husband would be at the party. And his new wife. And their kid.

So Jacqueline took the night shift.

She swallowed angrily, spinning back to face her computer.

I'm done. Free. So what if I don't make it to the Spring Fling? I don't need it. I could move out, today—well, not today, maybe tomorrow—or next week—and start my super amazing, dirty thirties lifestyle in the city. I'll live in an apartment, and drink cocktails with stupid names, and date, *and—*

The phone rang again and all the anger Jacqueline had held back while she was talking to the pizza woman exploded. She snatched up the phone.

"This had better not be another—"

The line crackled so loudly Jacqueline pulled the phone away from her ear. She squeezed her eyes shut. *Stay calm. Stay professional. Even that angry pizza lady is probably just pissed because she has to babysit while everyone else is at the Fling.*

The phone hissed and popped, and then a male voice quavered:

"Hello?... calling... Hideaway..."

Jacqueline's heart sank. *Is someone seriously calling to complain about the curse?* Complaining about the weather was one thing, but...

She sighed. Most people she knew joked about their neighboring town being responsible for any problems they faced—everything from late buses to, yep, electrical problems after storms—but calling to lodge a complaint with the sheriff was going too far, surely?

"Sorry, sir, can you repeat that please?"

"Trying to call—is this Hideaway? Got the number from…" His voice crackled and faded out.

Jacqueline rubbed her forehead. Not a curse complaint, then; just another crossed wire. "I'm sorry, sir, this is the Dunston sheriff's office. I can try to transfer you…" *And it'll probably go through to the pizza place, knowing my luck.*

"No, I… trying to get to… left them… storm…"

Jacqueline frowned. The voice on the other end of the line was male. His voice was deep, but it kept cracking, going up and down and wobbling with tension. Either she was imagining it, or the phone line was so bad it was making her hear things… or this guy was scared.

Alarm bells started going off in her head, but she forced her voice to remain calm.

"Sorry, sir, could you please repeat that?"

There was another burst of static, and then: "I'm sorry. I'm sorry, I didn't know what to do, but I left them there and now I can't get back, the road's closed and none of the buses are running and my car won't start and I can't get back to them—"

"To who?"

"I thought they'd be safe there, they're only… too small… left them… marine reserve. Trying… get to Hideaway but I couldn't call and now…"

Jacqueline's heart dropped. *Too small? Is he talking about children?* "I— you're saying you left someone at a marine reserve? During the *storm*?"

She could have hit herself. *Stupid.* Her job was to get the details and keep the caller on the line until she could get hold of someone to take action—not to berate them for whatever had made them call.

Especially not if there were children involved. Jacqueline's stomach clenched. She knew better than this. She couldn't let her own situation affect her professionalism.

"Sir, I understand if you don't want to leave a name, but if you could let me know where you are—we'll do whatever we can to help—"

9

She thought he started to say something else, but then there was a roar like a huge engine—*Or a storm*—and the call cut out.

Jacqueline stared at her computer screen.

The call logger will have the details of the call, the organized, sober part of her brain reminded her, but she couldn't focus on it. Her mind was miles away, in the open, exposed marine reserve that must have borne the brunt of the last week's storms.

She took a deep breath and glanced out the station's front window. The massive storms had broken windows and torn down tree branches here. What might they have done out on the wild coast?

Her hands moved automatically, probably because they had noticed her brain wasn't capable at the moment. They picked up her mobile and called her boss.

The call rang. And rang.

"Hi, this is Reg—"

"Boss, thank God. I've just had a distress call, I think, and it sounds like—"

"—probably a bit busy at the moment, so leave a message and I'll get back to you. Brent out."

Shit. Jacqueline grimaced. Answerphone. Of course. Because God forbid Reg actually take the "on call" part of his job seriously when there was punch and a live band on offer.

She took a deep breath and waited for the beep.

"Hi. Boss. This is Jacqueline. We've had a call reporting possible child abandonment at the marine reserve, up the coast. I'm going to go check it out. I'll have my mobile with me if you need me."

The office seemed to ring with silence as she ended the call.

I'm going up the coast.

Of course she was. There was no way she could take that call, hear the panic in the guy's voice, and not follow up. If it wasn't a prank, and he'd actually for whatever reason left some kids at the marine reserve...

She got up quickly, sending her office chair spinning away.

"It's probably just some teenagers having a joke," she told herself out loud. Her voice echoed around the empty office.

Good job, Jacqueline. You can't even convince yourself.

CHAPTER TWO
Arlo

*A*rlo furled the sails, letting the *Hometide* slip gently through the swell as the wind whipped through his hair. The sun had set, and soon the night would be so dark that the water turned black, nothing to separate it from the heavy canopy of sky. It was too cloudy for the moon to show, let alone any stars. The sailboat would seem to be drifting in space, only the distant lights on the coastline a reminder that the rest of the world existed.

Even those few lights grated against Arlo's skin. Later in the season, when the weather was more reliable, he'd sail further, away from the towns, away from streetlights and the glowing windows of people's homes. Until it was just the sea, and the sky, and him. Maybe then he'd be able to get his head right.

Arlo cursed and tied off the sail. The storms that had kept him landed for the last week had disappeared like smoke overnight, and he'd left Hideaway before first light, sliding out of the bay on still waters with his tail between his legs.

And he didn't even know *why.*

Everything had been going fine. Work was good, and Arlo's best friend Harrison had been preening like a peacock ever since he put a rock on his mate Lainie's finger.

Even Lainie's plan to build more houses in Hideaway Cove was going well. Arlo was proud to be a part of the project. More houses meant more homes for shifters, and that was what Hideaway Cove was all about. Shifters always looked after their own.

He, Harrison and the other builder on their crew, Pol, had celebrated the completion of the first house in the project the night before the storm hit. They'd broken out a few beers. Lainie had abstained, with a meaningful look at Harrison, and Pol had ribbed them both about how at least they'd finished their own house first, and then turned to Arlo and made a joke about which one of them would be next, and Arlo had been in a foul mood ever since.

Hrngg? his wolf whined, and Arlo sighed.

"Yeah, I know, buddy. It doesn't make any sense. Blame it on the weather."

The storm had hit that night—a first strength-test for the new build and a trial and a half for the headache that started pounding at Arlo's skull the moment Pol suggested he might be the next to find his mate. On a whim that he didn't understand, Arlo had asked Lainie how sales of the new sections on Lighthouse Hill were going. The build they'd just finished was spoken for, but he'd thought—he didn't know what he'd thought. His head had felt like someone was scraping it out with a rusty spatula, and when Lainie had reassured him that there were still sections available, he'd felt even worse.

I don't need a new house, anyway. I have the Hometide, *and a room above the workshop. Why do I need anything else?*

And why would that give me a headache, anyway? Or the idea of finding a mate? Hideaway's my home. Creating a family here, bringing them into the

13

Sweets' pack, would be the best thing to ever happen.

His head throbbed.

No, that can't be it. It must have been the weather change coming in. It was ludicrous to think that the unease coiling in Arlo's stomach and pounding at his skull might be because he was worried about finding his mate.

A spray of salt water burst over the port side of the boat and Arlo jerked, automatically scanning the water for what could have caused the disturbance.

He couldn't see anything; even the distant lights from the nearest human town were barely a glow on the horizon, and he was far enough from Hideaway that he couldn't sense any of his shifter friends or neighbors.

But, just in case...

He sent out a cautious telepathic signal. *Hello?*

There was no reply. Arlo relaxed. Just a stray wave. He was alone out here. Just him and his migraine.

God knows what I'd do if someone did pop by and want a chat, he thought glumly. *Bite their head off, probably.*

He released the anchor, trying to transform the relief he'd felt at realizing he was still alone into real relaxation. It didn't work. The headache was like a hammer, beating hot, sharp knocks on the back of his head. Constant. Frustrating. It was like...

It's like someone's trying to get my attention.

Arlo's shoulders tensed. He tentatively extended his shifter powers, checking for any telltale echoes of other shifters in the area. Nothing.

He shook his head and winced as it throbbed.

Nothing. Nothing certain, at least. Just a hint, a suggestion, of someone at the other end of the constant thudding in his head.

Arlo growled. *This had better not be one of Jools' pranks...* But, no, that wouldn't be like her. Jools' jokes were stupid, but they never hurt anyone.

This was something new. Or some*one* new.

Arlo groaned. He'd slipped out of Hideaway before dawn to avoid having to talk to anyone, not to trip over a new arrival and play welcoming committee.

A *lost* new arrival, apparently. Hideaway Cove was miles away, and that would explain why they were knocking on his skull like it was a door and they were after directions.

He'd dropped anchor as he debated with himself, and the boat swung towards the coast with the movement of water. It wasn't much, a few yards closer to land, but it was enough.

The psychic attack hit him like a sledgehammer. He sprawled over the deck, gasping.

Shit. Shit, shit, shit. Ignoring this wasn't a possibility.

He threw himself back at the anchor and began to raise it. Sails—he needed to let the sails down. Set a course for land. The clamor in his head almost blinded him and he squinted through streaming eyes.

It hurt. God, it hurt. Almost beyond bearing.

He should turn back. Find Harrison. Harrison would deal with this better than he could. Arlo was sure to fuck it up—if he even got there in time and didn't pass out from the pain.

But he couldn't. There might not be time. He couldn't even look at the point on the coast he was aiming at. It seemed to shimmer, crackling with the weight of the psychic force coming from it.

He couldn't have done anything else. He knew the emotions roaring like wildfire out across the water. It wasn't an attack—not a deliberate one, at least.

It was fear, and sorrow, and confusion. And loneliness so sharp it felt like a knife twisting in his gut. He'd been there before. It was too familiar.

But that wasn't what made him urge his boat faster toward the shore. That sheer force of telepathic power, the solid weight of emotion carried with it... he couldn't imagine any adult shifter being so open.

The headache that had been plaguing him all day, the wall of pain and fear—it was a shifter child, crying out for help.

15

CHAPTER THREE
Jacqueline

Jacqueline hissed through her teeth as the car's back wheels slid on slick black mud. The coastal road out to the marine reserve was a twisting, broken-up mess at the best of times, but it had taken an extra beating in the latest storms—and the town hadn't sent anyone out to fix things up yet.

Or ever, Jacqueline thought, narrowing her eyes at the road ahead. *That—oh, come on. I remember that slip from last time I was out here... how many years ago?*

Jacqueline shook her head as she counted back. Not since she'd started working at the sheriff's office, at least. A few years into her marriage.

Too long.

The marine reserve was quiet and peaceful, but Jacqueline was in no mood to appreciate it today. It had taken her over an hour to get this far, but she had slowed down to a crawl the last half-mile as the condition of the road got worse and worse. And what she could see in her headlights didn't exactly encourage her.

She eased around a slippery bend and groaned. A landslide covered the road.

And here I am in a two-wheel drive like some useless townie. If Reg hadn't taken the truck to cart everyone to the party...

Jacqueline tightened her grip on the steering wheel. *No turning back now.*

Reg hadn't returned her call. She didn't know if he'd even got her message. Either way, this was up to her.

Wincing, she trundled closer to the rocky, silty landslide. The car's front wheels spun and spun—and gripped.

"Yes!" she shouted. "Let's do this!"

She made it another ten feet.

The car's efforts didn't end with a bang, or a crunch. It just sank slowly into the sodden dirt, wheels whining as they spun.

"Drat!" Jacqueline snapped, smacking the steering wheel. "Useless—freaking—ugh!"

She wrestled the door open and took stock. The car was sunk halfway up the wheels.

So I'll have to call a tow truck. What'll that set me back? A few nights of cocktails?

Jacqueline squelched around the car and grabbed her handbag from the trunk, slinging it over her shoulder and stomping awkwardly over the last of the slip. Her flashlight made a sad, small circle of light on the mud.

The caller's panicked voice echoed through her mind. She pulled her phone out of her bag and slipped it into her bra. *Just in case Reg gets back to me. Or a call comes through from the office.* She'd set up an auto-forward before she left, although she wasn't sure how much she trusted it what with all the electrical weirdnesses lately.

A light breeze made her shiver. It was almost pitch black by the time she made it to the parking area at the entrance to the reserve. Jacqueline swung her flashlight around.

There wasn't much to see. Just an empty parking lot and a concrete building with its doors and windows boarded up. The lights of a boat blinked out on the water. She couldn't tell in the darkness what type of boat it was, or how far away.

Whoever they are, I hope they're having a better night than me.

Jacqueline frowned at the concrete building. When she'd been at school, her parents had told her that when *they* were at school, the old building had been used for field trips. Jacqueline couldn't remember ever seeing it without its doors and windows boarded up.

She let her flashlight linger over one of the boarded-up windows. Some of the wooden slats had been broken away.

Was that the storm, or...?

Hairs prickled on the back of Jacqueline's neck. She told herself it was just the cold.

Beyond the abandoned building was a boardwalk, leading out over the shallows and rockpools.

Given the state of everything else out here, that's probably rotten, too. Jacqueline looked around. There was no sign of anyone, but—she ran her flashlight over the broken boards on the window again.

Just in case...

"Hello?" she called out. Her voice carried on the chill air. "Is there anyone there? It's okay, you can come out. Your friend called me, he wanted me to come check up on you."

There was no reply.

A gull cried in the distance. Jacqueline shivered. The sea breeze was growing stronger, filling her lungs with the taste of brine, and now that the sun had set, the already brisk air was becoming chilly. It wasn't raining, but... Jacqueline looked up. Clouds. Which meant rain might still be on the agenda.

Wrapping her arms around herself, she walked out into the middle of the parking area.

"If there's anyone out there… your friend asked me to come look for you. I've got food, and blankets back in the car—I work for the sheriff, I'm here to help you."

She bit her tongue. Come to think of it, that might not be the best tactic to take with a group of runaway-or-lost kids. *Hey, kids! I'm with the sheriff! You're all sure in trouble now!*

Again, there was no reply. Jacqueline looked around, uncertain. There was no sign of any children.

Maybe it was a prank after all, she thought. *Ha, ha. Very funny. Thank God.*

She tipped her head back and closed her eyes. Her car was stuck in a muddy ditch, she'd ruined her shoes, and the news that she'd got herself into a tizz over some prank caller was going to be headline news in the office come Monday… but just for a moment, she stood and enjoyed the cool, fresh air on her face.

What with the storm, she'd been cooped up inside all week. And even if she hadn't been—when was the last time she'd been up the coast?

I used to love the water, she thought with a sigh. *Swimming, fishing, going out on a boat or body board, even if I had to wear a head-to-toe wetsuit to keep from freezing. What happened?*

She absently rubbed the empty spot on her ring finger.

It was beautiful. Peaceful. The clouds above made the night sky look soft and endless, like a huge ink-blue blanket over the world. There was the soft shush of the waves in the distance, and—

A shout echoed through the air and was suddenly cut off.

Jacqueline's eyes shot open. She spun on the spot, ears straining as she faced the direction she thought the shout had come from.

The boardwalk.

She broke into a sprint, the light from her flashlight zig-zagging madly ahead of her as she ran. The boardwalk was slick with seawater and she almost skidded over, grabbing the railing just in time. Panting, she swung the flashlight around, trying desperately to find the source of whoever had shouted.

Or whatever. No. The voice had been human. High-pitched, almost a yelp—but human.

She was sure of it.

Jacqueline squinted, forcing herself to search the area thoroughly, and not just whip the flashlight randomly around. Light glittered off the waves and the water swirling through the rockpools at the edge of the coast, and off a pair of dark eyes half-hidden in a pile of boulders.

Jacqueline froze. Then she blinked, and the dark shadow around the gleaming eyes solidified into a small seal, hiding in the rocks.

"Oh, shoot. I am such an idiot," she muttered.

That short, cut-off yelp—it could have been a seal, couldn't it?

She let the flashlight swing sideways, not wanting to disturb the seal any more than she already had. Just a seal. The call had been a prank after all, just as she—

"Oh no," she gasped, the blood in her veins turning to ice.

The beam of her flashlight was illuminating the rocks right at the edge of the water, where the rockpools turned into open water. Perched on the top of one of the rocks, with waves breaking over her head, was a little girl.

Jacqueline gaped. The girl was butt naked, with a tangle of curly hair that looked white-blonde in the light from her flashlight.

The girl waved and grinned when she saw Jacqueline staring at her. Then she yelped as another wave broke behind her, swamping her with salt spray.

"Oh sh—hey, hey kid!" Jacqueline was moving before the words left her mouth. "Just stay there, I'll come and get you! Don't move!"

If she falls in the water—

Jacqueline cut the thought off sharp. *Not going to happen.*

She ran further along the boardwalk. A plank gave way under her foot and she stumbled, losing one of her shoes. Behind her, the seal barked again.

Jacqueline wobbled to her feet and kicked off her other shoe. She was as close to the little girl as she could get on the boardwalk, but there was still twenty feet of broken rock and treacherous water between them. She glanced further out to sea; the boat was still out there, but too far away to help, even if they heard her shouting. She was on her own.

Jacqueline steadied her flashlight and gulped.

"Hey, honey!" she called out, holding the flashlight so she could see the girl without blinding her. The girl was still crouched on the same rock, but the waves were crashing too close behind her for comfort. "I'll be with you in a sec, okay? Just sit tight."

Jacqueline stepped gingerly out onto the rocks. They were jagged, but not slippery. She took a few tentative steps and then became more confident.

"Okay, Jacqueline. You can do this," she muttered to herself as the seal started barking more loudly. "Save the girl. Leave the local wildlife in peace. Attagirl."

She was less than six feet away from the girl when she stepped on what she thought was a rock and found herself hip-deep in icy, sucking water, surrounded by ropes of clinging seaweed. Pain shot through her foot as it landed on something sharp.

"Ah-h," she gasped, and grappled for a hold on the rocks before the water swept her off her feet.

A wordless shout echoed across the rocks. Jacqueline glanced over her shoulder to see—*You've got to be kidding me*—another curly-haired kid following her. A boy, maybe nine or ten, and just as naked as the little girl.

"Stop!" she called out. "Go back to shore!" *And—put some pants on! What the hell? Have I stumbled on some sort of hippie commune?*

Jacqueline turned back to the little girl, trusting the boy would listen to her. *The last thing I need is two kids falling in—*

Panting, she tried to haul herself up and slipped back again. The tide

21

sucked at her legs.

Shaking sea spray out of her eyes, Jacqueline raised her flashlight and checked on the girl. She was still there, and only a few feet away—but there was a deep pool between them. Dark water rushed through a gap in the rocks, treacherously fast.

If I can hardly hold myself up in this *current... then that one's gotta be bad. Really bad.*

Jacqueline looked across at the girl, whose face was creasing unhappily. "Hey, hey. It's okay, sweetheart. You just stay there and I'll come get you, okay? We can get you home—"

A decisive bark echoed across the rocks from back near the boardwalk. Jacqueline yanked herself up, managing to pull herself out of the water this time. She was measuring the gap—could she risk jumping across, or did she have time to find another way across?—when the girl stood up.

"No, no, honey, stay sitting down, the waves are—" Jacqueline began, and then her voice cut off.

I can't be seeing this. It's... no way. No way this is happening.

At first she thought the shimmering around the little girl was sea spray catching the light from her flashlight. Then the girl stretched out her arms, laughed, and *changed.*

Her tangled blonde hair disappeared, dark fur sprouted from her face and body, and a moment later there wasn't a little girl standing on the rocks. There was a seal pup.

Jacqueline swayed, dazed. A seal pup. That little girl had just changed... into a baby seal.

Part of her brain remembered the seal she'd seen hiding behind the rocks near the boardwalk... and the boy who'd appeared as though out of nowhere.

This isn't a prank, she thought wildly. *This is—this is—*

She blinked hard, as though it would change what she saw in front of her.

Why did the guy on the phone want to call Hideaway *about this?*

She opened her mouth, with no idea of what she was about to say—and then the pup overbalanced, yelped, and slid headfirst into the water.

Jacqueline didn't stop to think. She jumped.

Icy water closed over her head. The ocean was like a hand, wrapping around her and dragging her down. She dropped her flashlight and it spun around in the water, blinding her—but there, a darker shadow, seal-pup-sized. Jacqueline kicked wildly towards it.

The flashlight flickered out and she couldn't see anything, not even her own hands in front of her, but her fingers brushed something soft and she pulled the tiny creature into her arms and her knee hit something hard and she hoped it was the bottom, she hoped she was kicking off in the right direction because she had no way of telling what way was up or down and—

Air. Jacqueline gasped and flailed one hand until she hit rock. She grabbed it and pulled herself up, twisting her body so she wouldn't squash the seal pup—the little girl—the seal pup—*What is going on*—

A wave crashed over her head. Jacqueline pulled herself further up the rock.

"Hey kid," she gasped, then coughed out a mouthful of saltwater. The seal pup wriggled against her chest. "It's going to be—"

Someone shouted. It sounded close. Jacqueline raised her head. If that boy had come out after her—

Another wave hit, and she lost her grip on the rock. The water pulled her away and under.

CHAPTER FOUR
Arlo

"No!"

The young shifters' shouts echoed in Arlo's mind as he threw himself into the water.

His fault. He'd shouted when he was close enough to see what was happening, and the woman had lifted her head to look around. And the next wave had taken her.

She and the child had disappeared under the surface as though they had never existed.

I should have been faster. I shouldn't have distracted her. I should have—

Arlo forced the thought from his mind.

The water was cruelly cold. His wolf reveled in it, staking its strength and agility against the power of the sea.

Arlo strained his eyes and ears, ignoring the salt burn as he searched the water. It was pitch black, but the tiny shifter's telepathic shrieks were more than enough for Arlo to locate her.

There—the sea had pulled them away, but the next swelling wave might dash them against the rocks again. He swam towards them, his strong strokes cutting through the water like a hot knife through ice.

The woman jerked as he grabbed hold of her. A bubble of surprise burst against his chest and then she clutched at him. He pulled them both to himself, his arm around the woman, the pup sandwiched between them.

His feet slammed against the rocks at the bottom and he kicked, launching himself upwards. Sea spray battered his face as he broke the surface and the woman in his arms sucked in breaths, so hard it sounded like she was sobbing.

Their mouths were inches apart. Their breaths mingled, and something in the back of Arlo's mind went *ping.*

His wolf bristled with urgency. *Get her safe! Now!*

The seal's heart beat like a tiny drum against his chest and without thinking about it he sent out a telepathic burst of emotion. No words, just feelings, as instinctive as the young shifters' cries. Comfort. Safety. Protection.

He hadn't communicated with anyone like that in decades, with primal, instinctual emotion. Not since… a long time ago.

There was no time to think about that now. His rowboat was bobbing in the waves a few feet away; he swam towards it and grabbed hold of the side.

The woman coughed out a mouthful of seawater. "We'll tip it—"

"I'll hold the other side while you climb in," he told her. His wolf whined, impressed. She'd almost drowned, but she'd still kept her head enough not to try to clamber on board the rowboat and flip it over in the process.

"Wait! The girl first," the woman gasped. Then her eyes widened and she twisted to look back at the rocks. "There was another kid—oh, God, if he's—"

Arlo swept the shoreline. He could hardly sense anything past the tiny seal's psychic shrieks of excitement, but whoever was on shore, they weren't hurt or panicked. Just confused. Worried.

"He's fine," he reassured the woman, and made a silent promise to make sure that was true. He sent out a psychic warning to whoever else was out there to stay safe while they got ashore.

"Oh. Good."

The child shifter's confusion popped against Arlo's mind as the woman lifted her up over the side of the rowboat. She flailed against the woman's attempts to put her on board. Arlo trod water, keeping the woman and boat steady and sending reassurance to the little girl until she let herself be safely deposited inside the boat.

"Now you," he said firmly.

"Right…"

Arlo hauled himself hand-over-hand to the other side of the rowboat and called that he was ready. The woman took a deep, shaking breath and Arlo's heart froze.

Then she muttered something under her breath, kicked up and pulled herself over the side. She rolled into the boat with a clatter and a bitten-off curse.

The seal pup wobbled over her and was trying to clamber into her lap before she was even sitting upright.

"Okay. Okay, this is all… hey, honey, hey, there you are. Don't worry. It's all right. Everything's going to be all right."

Happiness bubbled across Arlo's mind as the woman picked the seal pup up and cuddled her. Despite himself, he smiled. Shifter kids that young shared their emotions with everyone nearby. The little girl's joy was infectious.

"There has to be a light here somewhere," the woman muttered. "What do you think, sweetheart? Are we going to find a light?"

"Should be under the seat," Arlo called.

"Got it. Watch your eyes." Arlo looked away and heard a *click* as she turned on the lantern. White light turned the water around the boat into a cauldron of stars. "Oh, that's better."

Her voice was clearer, no longer shaking with shock—but she had to be freezing.

Arlo looked up, but her face was hidden in shadows cast by the harsh light.

"Ready for me to come up?" he called, and the woman shifted her weight to the opposite side of the boat.

"Go on," she said, and Arlo pulled himself aboard.

Even though she was balancing the boat, Arlo weighed more than her and the scrap of a seal pup combined, so the boat rocked as he climbed aboard. The woman reached out to steady him, one arm still safely around the pup.

Arlo got his footing and looked up, about to tell her he was fine, he spent more time on the water than on land—and then their eyes met, and his mind went blank.

She was—she was…

She was leaning too far forward, her hand on his shoulder, and the boat was rocking. Her foot slipped and she fell toward him.

Arlo grabbed her and pulled her onto the seat next to him. There was hardly enough space; she was pressed in tight against him. No, not just pressed in. She was leaning against him, gasping with the cold.

Arlo wrapped one arm around her shoulder, the other over her hands. Her fingers were cold. He knew he should say something, but his throat was too tight.

His eyes strained like a drowning man reaching for the surface, calling on his shifter abilities to improve his sight. He felt like a man on the edge of a precipice. He felt like he was going to jump. Then the lantern rolled in the bottom of the rowboat, illuminating them both.

Her hair was flattened against her head, dark red made darker by the water. Her face was pale with cold and shock, her lips parted as she caught her breath, dark circles around her eyes where her make-up had smeared. And her hazel eyes caught Arlo like a fish in a net.

Warmth blossomed inside Arlo despite the cold air and colder water. For half a heartbeat, he thought the feelings of love and homecoming were coming from the little bundle in the woman's arms. A young shifter, reacting instinctively to a kind touch.

That lasted until he breathed in, and the woman's scent filled his senses.

The emotions he was feeling weren't the seal shifter's.

They were his.

He wasn't in the water anymore, he told himself. He had all the air he needed, even if his chest felt like there were iron bands around it.

His wolf was trembling with excitement inside him, but his human side...

It should have been wonderful, it should have been the best thing that ever happened to him, but instead the same nausea that had hit him back at the building site struck him like lightning: *This can't be happening. Not now.*

This woman was his mate.

He tightened his grip on the woman's hand. "You're—"

Human.

Oh, hell.

CHAPTER FIVE
Jacqueline

"Are you all right?" The man's voice was strange, almost choked. Jacqueline looked up quickly. Christ, if he'd inhaled half the ocean saving her and was about to fall over with secondary drowning…

"I," she began, and then she was the one swallowing her words. "I, um, yes. Fine. Thank you."

The seal pup snuffled and dove into her elbow. She repositioned her arms around it absently, still staring at the man who'd saved her life.

Mary mother of God, he was the hottest man she'd ever laid eyes on.

Not just literally, although heat poured from his body, as though he was hiding a furnace under—Jacqueline gulped. Not under his clothes, because he was barely wearing any. A worn shirt clung to his shoulders and biceps like it had been painted on, and hung open in front to reveal a muscular chest that gleamed and glittered in the light from the small lantern. His pants were low-slung enough that…

Jacqueline raised her eyes quickly.

Water streamed from his dark, curly hair, too, dripping over his forehead.

He blinked a droplet away and suddenly Jacqueline couldn't look away from his eyes.

His eyelashes were dark and thick, surrounding eyes the color of the night sky, and he was staring at her with an intensity she hadn't experienced since... since...

"I'm f-fine," she repeated. The bench seat they were sitting on was very small, she realized. Too small for both of them really. Her hip and thigh were pressed tight up against his.

The man's eyes flicked down her body and darkened. "You'll freeze, wearing that."

"Really, I don't feel cold at all," Jacqueline replied automatically.

She glanced down at herself and bit back a grimace. The nice dress she'd picked out for the Spring Fling hadn't exactly fared well against the might of the Pacific Ocean. It was flattened against her body, rucked up and twisted from when she'd clambered into the boat. And—oh, God, how could she not have noticed it riding up *that* far?

Jacqueline tugged at the hem and managed to at least cover the tops of her thighs before the little seal pup started wriggling enough that she had to turn her attention back to it.

"Hey, hey, it's all right. I bet you're not cold, huh, with that lovely fur coat." she cooed to it. It snuffled at her, gazed at her with its big wet eyes, and then dove back into her elbow.

The man made a stifled sound like a groan. When she looked up, he was grimacing.

He caught her eye and looked away. "Let's get in to shore," he muttered. Without looking at her, he gestured at the oars. "I'll need to..."

"Oh. Yes. Sorry." Jacqueline moved to the bench opposite. It was still a close fit, their knees almost touching across the gap—but it was an *almost* touch, not a squeezed-so-close-I-can-feel-you-breathe touch.

Jacqueline let out a slow breath.

She had been telling the truth. She *didn't* feel cold. But she'd just dived headfirst into the ocean. It might technically be spring but no one had told the water that. She should be freezing, and the fact that she wasn't feeling it now wasn't a good sign.

"Mrrf!" The seal pup squeaked into her elbow. "Mrrf!"

"We'll be there in a minute," the man said, "and you can tell me all about it."

"I didn't say anything," Jacqueline replied, and he gave her a guarded look.

"Well. Yes," he muttered, and hauled on the oars. The sight of his muscles working in the lantern light was almost enough to distract Jacqueline from wondering who he'd been talking to, then.

She looked down at the warm bundle in her arms.

I did see what I saw, didn't I?

Except it was… just a seal pup. And people didn't turn into animals, that was crazy talk.

Doubt began to wriggle at the edge of her mind.

The rowboat crunched against gravel, and the man was already halfway out of the boat by the time Jacqueline looked up. He reached out a hand and, after a brief wrangle with her own mind over whether he could possibly have any other reason for doing so, Jacqueline took it.

His hand was calloused, but gentle. A rush of warmth found its way to Jacqueline's cheeks. In the water, his arms around her hadn't been noticeably gentle—but they'd been strong. The moment he'd touched her she'd grabbed on to him. Even before they'd broken the surface she'd felt safe in his arms.

You mean you grabbed on to him as a drowning reflex, she corrected herself. *And then stayed so clingy he had to literally tell you to back off so he could reach the oars.*

She sighed, then winced as she stepped out of the boat. The man's grip might be gentle, but the stony shoreline was anything but. She grimaced and tiptoed up to the relatively foot-safe concrete by the old building.

"Ow," she muttered, shaking off a piece of gravel that had gotten lodged—yes, in the tattered remains of her pantyhose.

There was a shout behind her, and a low bark. Jacqueline spun around to see...

Nothing.

She narrowed her eyes. The lantern was still on the boat, and only a little of its light filtered this far up the beach. But she was sure she'd seen *something*. A flash of movement.

"Who's out there?" she called. There was no sign of the boy she'd seen on the rocks earlier. "Kid? You don't need to hide. I already saw you, remember?"

A clatter of falling rocks closer to the boardwalk caught her attention, and she turned just in time to see another big fat nothing in the shadows.

"I just want to know for sure you're all right," she said, pitching her voice to carry into the shadows. "Your friend who called me, he was really worried about you."

"Why would Eric call you? You're human."

Jacqueline spun around. The boy she'd seen earlier was standing just a few feet away. He'd found some clothes, thank goodness, and was wearing a pair of stained sweatpants and a thick sweater, with a ragged backpack slung over his shoulders.

"You say 'human' like there's another option," she said carefully, and the seal pup in her arms gave an impatient wriggle.

The boy's eyes went wide. "There isn't!" he exclaimed. "Um, but, do you want me to take her? It? The seal. I'm... studying them? For school?"

"Uh-huh." Jacqueline was unconvinced, but the seal pup started wriggling more as the boy reached out and she decided to hand it over. The boy got a football grip on the pup and hunched over it, whispering.

"What's your name?" Jacqueline asked.

"Dylan," he replied absently, and then: "No, don't! Not now!"

"Let me take her!" Another figure darted out of the shadows. This one was a young woman with her hair in a messy braid. Jacqueline guessed she was in her early teens.

The girl gave Jacqueline a suspicious glare and took the seal pup.

Jacqueline crossed her arms. "So you're studying the local seal population too, huh?"

"I'm—" The girl glared at Jacqueline and closed her mouth with a scowl.

"We making introductions?" Jacqueline's mystery rescuer strode up from where he'd been pulling the rowboat above the waterline. "I'm Arlo." His eyes flicked to Jacqueline's, and away again. "Arlo Hammond."

His voice was a low rumble that seemed to reverberate through Jacqueline's bones. She shivered. "Jacqueline March."

Was she imagining it, or did his cheeks go slightly pink? No. She was making things up. *Crazy.*

"I'm Kenna," the teenaged girl admitted reluctantly. "Kenna Weaver. This is Dylan, and—"

She closed her mouth so quickly her teeth clacked together.

"All right. Kenna, Dylan, and Tally—uh, Jacqueline. Why don't you tell us what you're doing here?" Arlo cleared his throat and flashed Jacqueline a wary look.

An electric charge raced up her spine. *Okay, now I'm definitely suspicious. Tally? Who's Tally?*

She looked around the small group. Kenna and Dylan had to be brother and sister; they had the same wriggly blond hair and snub noses.

And then there was the seal.

And Arlo.

"I see," Arlo said, even though no one else had said anything. He took a heavy breath and ran one hand over his jaw.

"Wait, what's going on here?" Jacqueline demanded. "Dylan, you thought your friend—Eric—wouldn't call me because I'm human? And you both—" She flung up her hands. "What am I saying? Both of you? All *three* of you. That little seal was a little *girl* when I first saw her, I'm—I'm sure of it."

Are you? Doubt wormed at her. *Maybe you just* thought *you saw...*

She shook her head. "Either way, we need to get you back into town. I can organize a place for you to stay until we get everything sorted out."

"Get what all sorted out?" Kenna scowled. "You don't know anything about—no, not now!" Kenna made a frustrated noise as the seal pup wriggled around in her arms.

Jacqueline crossed her arms. "I know you've been staying out here for who knows how long, waiting for Eric to come get you. But he's not coming."

Kenna flinched, and Jacqueline immediately regretted being so blunt.

"He's really upset about that, but he wants you to be safe. And so do I, and that means not leaving you out here in the middle of nowhere. I can take you back to Dunston—"

"We're not going!" Kenna was scowling so fiercely Jacqueline was worried she was about to burst into tears.

Dylan was wincing, too. Even Arlo looked uncomfortable.

"What's going on?" she asked. "What am I missing?" Jacqueline's head was spinning. Maybe she was going into shock, after all. It was as though there was a conversation going on that she couldn't hear half of.

"Ms. March," Arlo began, and rubbed his jaw again with a wince. "I can explain."

He sounded so *reasonable.*

Jacqueline had met so many reasonable men. Especially these last few years. Derek had been perfectly reasonable when he told her there was nothing going on. Then he'd been just as reasonable when he told her he had a secret two-year-old, and that she didn't need to hire her own divorce lawyer, because didn't she trust him to do the right thing?

Arlo exchanged a glance with Kenna and Dylan and something inside Jacqueline snapped.

"Don't you dare lie to me." Jacqueline met Arlo's gaze, her heart in her throat. "I am so *sick* of people lying to me."

Please, she added silently. *Please, please don't lie. Don't tell me I'm crazy. Don't tell me I'm imagining things.*

She'd had more than enough years of that already.

CHAPTER SIX
Arlo

A shock of horror jolted down Arlo's spine.

She was right. He couldn't lie to her.

"Ms. March," he said, and her eyes narrowed suspiciously. "I won't lie to you. You deserve to know the truth, but—"

"But what?" Jacqueline had her arms folded tightly in front of her. Her shoulders hunched and Arlo saw a flicker of uncertainty pass across her face. "I saw—I *know* what I saw…"

I could use this, Arlo thought miserably. *It's what I'm meant to do in this situation, isn't it? What all Hideaway shifters are meant to do if a human suspects what we are. Use her uncertainty and confusion. Tell her she didn't see what she thought she saw. Keep our secret safe.*

But she'd sounded so desperate when she told him not to lie to her. And she was his mate. He had to trust her.

His head was pounding with the three shifter children's voices.

He can't tell her. Humans aren't meant to know about us!

But Eric called her—

Did he? Really? How do we know that? She said she works for the sheriff, she just wants to take us back to that stupid home and take Tally away again!

Tally whined and a buffet of an emotion that could only be described as "togetherness" hit Arlo like a sack of bricks. He swayed back.

No, Tally, that can't be—she can't be right, can she?

But you feel it too, right?

Hang on… no way…

Arlo shook his head as though he could shake their voices off. Hadn't anyone taught these kids to keep their private conversations private and not broadcast them for everyone to hear? At least Tally was young enough for that to be an excuse.

Kids, can you give it a rest? I can hardly hear myself think.

Kenna and Dylan both gasped, eyes wide. *You can hear us? He can hear us!*

Their voices suddenly fell silent, except for the constant waves crashing from Tally's mind. Arlo's shoulders sagged. *That's something, at least.*

He looked back at Jacqueline—his *mate*—who was glaring at him suspiciously.

His heart sank. *My mate is looking at me like she's ready for a fight. My mate. She just threw herself into danger to save this shifter child, and she's looking at me like I'm the last person in the world she would trust.*

"You're right," he said, his voice rougher than the rocks that stood hard against the crashing waves. "I won't lie to you. We're—"

"Tally *don't*—" Kenna yelped, but it was too late. Tally wriggled and shifted back into her human form.

Jacqueline's eyes went wide and she swayed back. Arlo froze, watching her. Waiting for her reaction.

"Oh," she breathed. "Oh, you—you *will* get cold like that, honey. Does one of you have another sweater for her?"

She's not scared, or disgusted. Arlo's heart lightened, and for some reason it hurt as well as felt good. *She just wants to look after her.*

Dylan pulled some more clothes from his bag with a flourish. While he and Kenna wrestled Tally into them, Jacqueline glanced up at Arlo, her eyes wide with wonder.

"I wasn't imagining it," she whispered. She took a step closer to him. "And you're not surprised by any of this. Are you?"

The air between them seemed to shiver with possibility. Arlo was vaguely aware of the kids clustering together and whispering between themselves, but he couldn't tear his attention away from Jacqueline.

37

"No," Arlo admitted before he could stop himself. "I'm like them."

A complicated, closed-off expression took hold of Jacqueline's face. Arlo's wolf whined: it didn't want closed-off. It wanted everything to be open and clear between them, and it wanted to be able to *help*. To drive away whatever was hurting her.

Arlo almost groaned at the effort it took to not simply throw himself at Jacqueline's feet and beg her to let him in.

"You can turn into a… seal?" Jacqueline asked.

"Not exactly." Arlo gazed into Jacqueline's eyes. His mind had this all twisted up, but his heart? His heart, and his wolf, knew what he needed to do. "I—"

Kenna Dylan wanna fish!

"I—"

Wanna fish fish FISH!

Arlo paused. Dylan had told him the toddler's name before using his megaphone-like telepathy.

Tally… he began—and then realized his mistake.

Tally stared at him. He felt her look at him, and then look deeper, into what he really was.

"I—" he tried again.

WANNA FISH WANNA PLAY WITH DOGGY—

No no no! Kenna's telepathic voice was much more on edge than her spoken voice. *No, she was like this just before she slipped away before. Dylan, make her stop!*

She already ate all the chocolate! Dylan yelled back. He looked like he might cry.

"Hey, it's not that bad," Jacqueline said. She put her arm around Dylan's shoulder and squeezed. "Everything's going to be fine, okay?"

"But she already ate *everything*," he whined, sagging against her.

Arlo shook his head. His temples were pounding. He shot an apologetic look at Jacqueline.

"I think these kids need their dinner, and I've got food on the *Hometide*."

Jacqueline's eyes slid past him, to his boat, moored out in the darkness. "Oh," she said, her voice listless. Arlo opened his mouth to speak, but then her whole body stiffened, as though she'd stepped on a live wire.

"I'm coming with you," she declared, her eyes blazing.

"Of c—" Arlo began.

"I'm not going to go home and pretend I never saw any of this. I *can't*."

Her voice broke on the last word, letting through a sliver of desperation. She caught her breath and Arlo felt like his heart had stopped as he waited for her to speak again.

She stared into his eyes as though she was searching for something. Arlo's chest tightened.

What does she see when she looks at me?

He knew the face that had looked out at him from the mirror that morning: hair a tangled mass of knots, stubble like he'd dipped the lower half of his face in a pile of iron filings, eyebrows that you could hide half a football team in.

She was beautiful, and he was… a mess. In more ways than one.

Jacqueline narrowed her eyes. "I'm not going *anywhere* until I know Kenna, Dylan and Tally are safe."

Good, Arlo's wolf huffed, satisfied. Arlo was bewildered at its reaction—and relieved.

Jacqueline took another deep breath. "If you're going to tell me this is none of my business—"

"I'm not." Arlo raised his hands in surrender. "I was going to say thank you. *Am* going to say thank you. I appreciate the help."

"Oh." The fight went out of her. "Um. Good. Because my car is stuck in a ditch about a half-mile back, and I don't expect my phone will have agreed with that little dip I took in the sea back there, so going with you is basically my only option here, anyway." Her shoulders dropped and the wan smile she gave him made his heart break.

If I'd lied and tried to get the kids away from her, I would have abandoned her here with no way to get home. Arlo's gut clenched. *There's no coming back from that.*

"We'd better get moving," he said. "No chance of sailing tonight, but there's warm clothes, and food."

"What else could we need?" Jacqueline said brightly.

Arlo's eyes trailed after her as they gathered up the kids' belongings and squeezed everyone into the rowboat.

What else? So much more. But I'm beginning to think I'm not the man who can give it to you.

CHAPTER SEVEN
Jacqueline

*A*rlo's boat was not what she'd expected. He was so salt-crusted and rough-looking, Jacqueline had thought he must have come off a working fishing boat, covered in shed scales and chased by seagulls.

Which only went to show she shouldn't make assumptions.

The *Hometide* was a sleek cutter, all oiled wooden boards and crisp sails. The water slapped against its sides as Arlo secured the rowboat and helped them all climb aboard. Jacqueline went up last, and his touch burned against her skin.

I really am cold, she thought, biting her lip. She flexed her fingers, testing them. How many times was it you were meant to be able to clench and unclench your fists, before it was time to be worrying about hypothermia? She was sure she'd known, once. Back when she spent more time outdoors than doing vacuuming in that huge empty house.

"There's clothes downstairs," Arlo said, appearing at her shoulder.

"What?" Jacqueline jumped, and he seemed to curl in on himself.

"Dry clothes. In the cabin downstairs. You look…" He looked away.

"Cold."

"And soaking wet," Jacqueline agreed, shaking out her arms. Arlo made a strange noise in the back of his throat.

"I'll show you."

The *Hometide* had a comfortable cockpit in the stern, fitted out with cushions on the seats and cup holders stuffed with sunscreen and water bottles. A wooden hatch with a round window led down into the cabin. Jacqueline climbed down the ladder after Arlo and he pointed behind it to a low-roofed alcove.

"Clothes in the cupboard. There should be a towel… I'll get dinner on."

His voice was rough, and Jacqueline bit back a sigh. He might have saved her life, but it was obvious he resented her presence here.

Too bad. She was going to see this through. She'd spent the last three years paralyzed by life. She'd almost frozen again, back there on the beach.

But she couldn't do that anymore. She had no excuses left for not *doing* anything with her life. And making sure this little family made their way to Hideaway to wait for the man she'd spoken to on the phone might not be the same thing as partying it up in a club, but at least it was something. It wasn't another Friday night at work or at home, terrified that she'd do something wrong and the rest of her world would come crashing down.

She waited until Arlo had gathered everything he needed from the small kitchen and then clambered into the alcove. Her knees sank into a mattress and she realized, too late, that the entire space was a bed.

Arlo's bed.

Jacqueline's face blazed. *I'm climbing into another man's bed*, she thought, stupidly, and even more stupidly felt a rush of guilt. She pushed it away, frowning.

What do I have to feel guilty about? Even if Arlo was interested in me— Derek left me. I don't have to feel bad about noticing other men exist.

She crawled over the bed to the cupboard set into the very stern of the cabin. There was something in the wall above the cupboard that looked like it should have been a window, but it was boarded over.

Another victim of the storm? Jacqueline wondered, and opened the cupboard.

Jacqueline pulled a shirt, sweater and pants from the cupboard and wriggled back into the main cabin. She glanced back at the bed—she'd left the covers a mess and that made her blush, too.

Oh, no. I have it bad, don't I? What timing, my first crush since...

She winced and pulled off her sodden dress. *Trust me to lose my head over another guy who couldn't care less.*

She scrubbed herself as dry as she could and pulled on fresh clothes. Arlo was so much bigger than her that she was sure she looked ridiculous—but at least she was warm. His woolen sweater enveloped her like a hug, warming her inside and out—

Oh, stop it, she told herself, and climbed back onto deck.

She was greeted by the smell of frying butter, and three pairs of nervous eyes. Kenna and Dylan both looked like they'd had a rug pulled out from under their feet, but Tally's main concern seemed to be whatever was happening over the small gas cooker.

Arlo was turned away, his attention all on the stove.

"I brought you up a sweater," Jacqueline said awkwardly, holding it out. "You're only in your shirt—I thought you might be cold..."

He paused before he took it. "Thanks."

Then he stripped off his wet shirt. Jacqueline closed her eyes. *Oh lord.*

"Shifters don't feel the cold, actually. We're really really tough."

Jacqueline opened her eyes to find Dylan grinning at her. His older sister, not so much. When Kenna saw her looking, she scowled and looked away.

"That's very interesting." Jacqueline sat down opposite them.

Despite what Dylan had just told her, she was pleased to see that while she was downstairs, someone had wrestled some clothes onto Tally, and all the children were in shoes and warm coats. She wriggled her bare toes and tucked them into the bottom of her over-long borrowed pants.

"Is that what you are? Shifters?"

"Yeah." Dylan sighed dramatically and leaned against his sister, who hunched down into her collar. "Don't be like that, Kenna, Mr. Hammond said we could tell her!"

"Not everything!" Kenna met Jacqueline's eye and then glared and stared at her hands.

She can't be more than twelve or thirteen, Jaqueline thought. *What is going on here? Where are their parents?*

And why do I keep feeling like I'm missing half the conversation?

Butter hissed as Arlo laid fish fillets in the pan. "There's bread and butter," he said over his shoulder. "Any of you want to—"

"Dylan will," Kenna said quickly, elbowing her brother.

"Hey!"

They certainly act like normal kids, Jacqueline thought as the two squabbled over who would cut and butter the bread. Her heart ached a little, but she ignored it. *Not the most important issue here, Jacqueline.*

By the time the fish was cooked, Jacqueline's stomach was rumbling. She'd planned to eat at the Spring Fling, but that hadn't happened—and she *hadn't* planned to jump headfirst into the ocean. Almost dying had an invigorating effect on the appetite, apparently.

Dylan and Arlo got a system going: Dylan handed Arlo a plate of bread and butter, Arlo put fish on top, and Dylan passed them out.

Tally's eyes were as big as saucers as she watched the plates go around. When Dylan put one in front of her, she leaped in with both hands.

"This looks delicious. Thank you," Jacqueline said to Dylan as he passed her a steaming plate.

The fish was melt-in-your-mouth delicate. Jacqueline closed her eyes as she took her first bite. The salted butter and fresh bread were better than any restaurant meal she'd ever had.

"Oh, man," she murmured, and wiped a smear of butter off her chin.

"This is…"

"It's not much." Arlo's voice was rough. "I wasn't expecting guests."

"I think this is the best thing I've ever eaten," Jacqueline said honestly, and took another bite.

Arlo's eyes burned into hers, and when he looked away, she was sure his cheeks were pink. "Good," he muttered.

Warmth bloomed inside her chest. Maybe he didn't resent her being here so much, after all. Except he kept wincing like he was in pain.

"Are you okay?" she asked tentatively. "You didn't get hurt back there in the water, did you?"

Oh geez. If I kicked him in the ribs or something while he was saving my life…

"It's nothing," Arlo said quickly, and winced again. He sighed and rubbed his forehead. "That is, it's a…"

He trailed off, and Jacqueline felt a tug on her sweater.

Tally had already finished her dinner and had wriggled down off her seat. When she saw Jacqueline looking at her, she raised her arms to be picked up.

"Come on then. You're not a big talker, are you?"

Jacqueline picked Tally up and arranged her on her lap. She looked up. Arlo, Kenna and Dylan were all wincing, now.

"What's wrong?"

"*Ugh*," Kenna said, and turned side-on in her seat so she wasn't facing Jacqueline and Tally.

Arlo tapped his forehead. "She's loud in here," he explained in response to what was probably an expression of utter confusion on Jacqueline's face. "Telepathy. Or mindspeaking, some call it. Shifters use it to talk when we're shifted, or…"

"When your mouth is otherwise occupied?" Jacqueline suggested. While her attention had been distracted, Tally had started to help herself to Jacqueline's plate, and now she was busily gnawing on a crust of bread.

45

Did she eat that whole slice while I wasn't looking? Jacqueline marveled. "Um… what's she saying?"

The corner of Arlo's mouth hooked up. Like a smile. Was he smiling at her?

"Before or now?"

"Now?"

He cleared his throat. "That would be something along the lines of: *Bready bready bread, yum yum bread, mmm bread I love you.*"

Jacqueline burst out laughing. "No. Seriously? And before?"

Dylan piped up. "Before she was saying *fish fish yum fish yum.* Over and over. She *really* likes fish."

"You're not kidding." Jacqueline's second fish sandwich was disappearing as fast as the first. First, Tally hoovered up the fillet, then she chomped through the soft bread until she was left with another crescent-moon crust. "Should I be sorry or glad that I can't hear her?"

"You're lucky," Kenna grumbled. "She *never* shuts up. She even sings in her sleep sometimes."

If this was a cartoon, I'd have hearts in my eyes right now. "Really?"

"I wish—" Kenna continued, and then frowned at her plate and fell silent. "Never mind."

Kenna and Dylan had both cleared their plates, which was lucky, because as soon as the last of the crust disappeared into Tally's mouth, she started looking around in interest. When she saw the others had already finished, she sighed, lay back, and promptly fell asleep in Jacqueline's lap.

One million heart-eyes, Jacqueline thought.

"You haven't eaten." Arlo's voice was gruff. Jacqueline gestured to the slumbering toddler in her lap.

"I didn't get much of a chance," she replied.

He frowned. "I'll get you—damn. That was the last of the bread."

Kenna frowned. "Tally…" she groaned.

"I'm okay, really. Don't worry about me." The last thing Jacqueline wanted was to make a fuss and have Arlo regret letting her on board.

"You're sure?"

"I'm not even hungry," Jacqueline lied. Her stomach gave a slight gurgle as she breathed in the remnant smell of buttered bread and hot fried fish, but luckily Tally gave a tiny snore at the same time, so she was almost certain no one would notice. "What about you two? Neither of you had as much to eat as your sister."

"That's because we have manners, actually," Dylan announced, kicking his legs. "But also she's growing a lot and she has to grow for her *and* her seal."

"And you two don't?"

"You're probably past that first growth spurt." Arlo raised an eyebrow at the two of them and got a vigorous nod from Dylan and a grunt and a shrug from Kenna.

"First growth spurt?" Jacqueline hadn't meant to look at Kenna, but she did, and the girl jumped like she'd sat on a bee.

"Shifters have our first growth spurt when we're, like, um, however old we are when we first shift, which for Tally is *really* early, because the seal needs a lot of energy to even exist that first time. And then we have normal human growth spurts or whatever and then it all settles down and we can pretend to be normal humans, if we're old enough."

Arlo wiped the cooking pan clean and added, "Not completely. We still have to eat more than normal humans do." He nodded at Jacqueline. "Our animal sides still need extra energy."

And I bet it takes a lot of energy to keep your body looking like that, Jacqueline thought. Her cheeks heated up and she looked down at Tally dozing in her lap. When she looked up again, Kenna was staring at her.

"You really don't know anything about shifters?" she asked. "But..." Her eyes flicked between Jacqueline and Arlo.

Arlo held up a reassuring hand. "Don't worry. She'll keep your secret. Won't you?"

"I won't tell anyone," Jacqueline said. "Promise."

"That wasn't what I meant," Kenna protested.

"Yeah, if you don't know about shifters, then how can you be—"

"Not that, Dylan!" Kenna hissed. She caught Jacqueline's look of confusion and bit her lip. "I mean, how did Eric know to call you if you're human?"

Jacqueline tugged on her sleeves to buy time. "I, er, I think he was just looking for anyone who could help you."

Kenna pursed her lips as though she didn't quite believe her. Jacqueline didn't blame her—but she wasn't ready to tell the truth just yet. Maybe it was selfish, but she didn't want this crazy adventure to end just yet.

Not before the kids were safe, at least.

Dylan was tugging on Kenna's shirt. "But what about…"

"We'll talk about that later!" Kenna shout-whispered back.

What's that about? Jacqueline exchanged a questioning look with Arlo, and he shrugged. Somehow, that helped. It couldn't be a mysterious shifter thing if Arlo didn't know what was going on, either. Just a mysterious kid-sibling thing.

"Do you have a phone out here?" she asked Arlo. "I should check in with my work. Let them know I'm okay and that I found the kids. And…" she added cautiously, "if there's anyone you need to call, Kenna, Dylan…"

"Like who?" Kenna was back to being surly.

"Any relatives, or…"

"There's just Eric," Kenna said sharply. "He's looking after us. I guess he's, like, our uncle."

"He's the one who left you on the beach?" Arlo growled.

Kenna's eyes flashed. "He's taking us to Hideaway Cove! Where we'll be safe! No one else—"

"Our parents died," Dylan said quietly.

"I'm so sorry." Jacqueline reached out for Dylan automatically and he wriggled over to her. Arlo put a hand on Kenna's shoulder and she sort of sagged into it.

"They were in a car crash," Dylan whispered.

"So it's just us." Kenna was scowling again and this time Jacqueline was convinced it was to stop herself from bursting into tears. "And we got put in a home, which was fine, except Tally started shifting early and they were going to find out."

"You have to keep yourself safe from humans." Jacqueline's heart dropped.

Kenna nodded angrily. "Eric told us about Hideaway Cove, he said we'd be safe there—"

"And you will be," Arlo rumbled. Jacqueline was struck by the certainty in his voice. "Hideaway Cove is a sanctuary for all shifters. You'll be safe there, and welcome, and cared for. Your whole pack." He paused and frowned. "Eric, too."

Dylan and Kenna exchanged a look. "Really? That's actually true?"

"One hundred percent." Arlo hesitated again, his eyes flicking to Jacqueline. She couldn't read the expression in them. "They took me in when I was just a bit older than you. I lost my family, too. Hideaway Cove gave me a new one."

Jacqueline let out a short breath. *So many broken pasts,* she thought, her heart aching.

"Anyway," Arlo muttered. "We've got an early start if we want to make it to Hideaway and call your work, Ms. March. There's no phone on board, I'm sorry. I'll just get this cleaned up—"

"I'll help!" Kenna said quickly.

"—and then we'd better pack in for the night. You kids can take the bed. Ms. March…" His voice went gravely, and Jacqueline felt another blush start to prickle across her skin. "The seat in the kitchen booth isn't much, but I can pull some extra blankets out."

"That'll suit me fine. But what about you?"

Jacqueline regretted asking the moment the words were out, because as soon as she'd spoken them, she was imagining Arlo in bed. His long body stretched out across the blankets. His head resting on one arm, his chest the perfect pillow just begging for her to...

Jacqueline squeezed her eyes tight. *What is wrong with me? He's made it clear he's not interested, anyway.*

...Which maybe makes this all right? There's nothing wrong with imagining, *right? And if it's not going to go anywhere...*

"I'll sleep up here," Arlo said, and Jacqueline's mind immediately filled in the dots.

"Er, won't you be cold?" she asked, mentally dodging the images her brain was throwing at her.

Arlo half-smiled. "I've got my own fur coat. I'll be fine."

"Oh. Yes. Of course." Jacqueline felt like she'd just stuffed her entire foot in her mouth. Her cheeks might as well have been on fire.

Tally was still asleep, so she stayed up on deck with Dylan while Arlo and Kenna dealt with the dishes. Dylan was full of questions about Hideaway Cove, most of which Jacqueline couldn't answer. Everything she knew about the town could have fit on the front of an envelope.

Everything true, at least. The rumors could have filled a phone book, but she wasn't about to tell Dylan that people back home thought Hideaway Cove was full of telephone-cursing witches.

Suddenly, Dylan sat up straight. "They're all done!" he chirped, and hopped over to the hatch.

"Be careful with that—and how do you know?" Jacqueline balanced Tally over her shoulder and got to the hatch just before Dylan hauled it open and, she suspected, threw himself headfirst down the steps.

"Arlo said." Dylan tapped the side of his head. "In here."

"Right. Well, go down backwards, okay? I don't want you to slip."

"Shifters don't *slip*," he said, and Jacqueline raised her eyebrows at him.

"Someone needs to tell Tally that, then," she said. "Before she *slips* off any more rocks."

"She's a baby! She doesn't count."

Jacqueline's eyebrows shot up. "Don't listen to him, honey," she said facetiously to the slumbering Tally, and Dylan cackled.

She held the hatch open as he clambered down, then climbed after him and found herself back-to-chest with Arlo.

"Oh," she said, stupidly, and turned around, also stupidly, because now she was still pressed against him, but in a way more awkward position.

Why, why, why hadn't she put her bra back on when she got changed?

She climbed a step back up the stairs, but that only put her boobs level with his eyes.

Arlo's eyes darted either side of her. "Excuse me," he muttered in his gravelly voice, and dodged around the ladder.

"It's small with us all down here, huh?" Jacqueline said, trying to ignore her blazing cheeks. "Cozy."

"Uh-huh." Kenna had scooted into the booth to get out of the way. "Um, you can have the bed, if you want. We've got fur coats, too, so we don't need—"

Jacqueline fixed her with a mock glare. "How long have you been camping out in that ancient concrete block?" she demanded.

"Um, a few weeks, I guess…"

"Then it's definitely your turn to sleep in a bed. I'll be fine on the bench."

"Here you go." Arlo grabbed an armful of extra blankets from the cupboard at the end of the bed. He handed a few to Jacqueline, and spread the others on the mattress, making a sort of nest on top of it. "It's a few hours down the coast to Hideaway. By lunchtime tomorrow, you'll be in your new home."

"Isn't that a bit—" *optimistic*, Jacqueline had been about to say, but managed to stop herself at the last minute. "Quick? I mean, I don't know how shifters do things, but they're just kids. Won't you have to wait until Eric is here to decide a place for them to live?"

Arlo shook his head. "This isn't the first time the town's taken in strays.

There'll be more than enough houses open to them until this *Eric* gets here. And anyway…"

He pressed his lips together, his eyes shadowing. Whatever he'd stopped himself from saying, it looked like an old hurt.

Dylan raised his head quizzically and Jacqueline decided to interrupt.

"And anyway, now that they're here there's no way you're letting them get away, right? No more camp-outs in derelict buildings."

"Exactly." Arlo flashed her a relieved smile and her heart lifted. Maybe this all was going to be all right after all. It wasn't the fling she'd been hoping for this weekend, but it was something. A tiny sliver of magic, and helping people, before she headed back to her own life.

Or whatever it was she was going to make of her life.

"No more baths in a sink," Kenna muttered. She caught Jacqueline's eye and blushed, her hand going to her tangled mop of hair.

"What's your house like?" Dylan piped up.

Arlo frowned. "My house?"

"Yeah, where we're going."

Arlo straightened. "Well, it's…" He ran his fingers through his hair and closed his eyes in a silent groan. Jacqueline thought she saw his lips moving as though he was saying something under his breath. "You know I'm not taking you to stay with me, right?"

Kenna folded her arms, her face settling into mutinous lines. "Then where are you taking us?"

"Well, maybe my parents—my foster parents. Dorothy and Alan Sweets. They're all set up with the county to take in kids that need a home. They'll look after you until Eric gets a place set up for you."

"But—" Dylan began, and Kenna shushed him. He stared at her, bewildered, and then turned to Jacqueline. "But what about…"

Jacqueline was confused. "Me?"

Dylan nodded, his eyes huge. Kenna growled something and Dylan swatted the air as though he was trying to bat away an invisible fly.

"I live in Dunston, not Hideaway Cove. I doubt you want to live there after everything you've been through to get to Hideaway," Jacqueline said, smiling, and Dylan's face fell.

"You're going back to Dunston? But I thought you and A—"

"Shut *up*, Dylan!" Kenna screamed, jumping to her feet. "Just *shut up* for once, will you?"

"Hey, now—" Arlo began, as Tally stirred in Jacqueline's arms and began to grizzle.

"But I thought we were going to—" Dylan's face creased with confusion.

"*Stop talking!*" Kenna bawled at him, pink spots spreading like a fever across her cheeks. "Stop—they—you can't just—and we—you're going to *ruin it!*"

Tally's grizzle blew into a full-out wail, and she kicked her legs like she was trying to swim out of Jacqueline's grip. Jacqueline got a better hold on her and just managed to fling her other arm in front of Kenna as she threw herself down the cabin towards Dylan.

Dylan's look of confusion morphed into mulish anger. "No, *you're* going to ruin it all, because *you're* yelling and you said humans couldn't—"

"*Shut up!*"

"So it'll be *your* fault anyway if—"

Jacqueline hadn't been able to hear what humans "couldn't" do over Kenna's shriek, but her heart was breaking for both of them.

There were so many times she'd wanted to scream her heart out over the last few years. She knew how much they were hurting, and how much more it would hurt when they'd all calmed down and remembered what they'd said.

Arlo was still bent over double in the bed nook. He raised his head and clonked it on the ceiling. "Ah, blast—Hey, kids, that's enough of that. Calm down."

Kenna's head snapped back like she'd been slapped, and her eyes filled with tears. She stared at Arlo, then Jacqueline, her mouth opening and closing like a goldfish. "I didn't mean—you can't—oh *no*…"

Behind her, Dylan's face creased. Arlo rubbed his forehead and groaned. "Damn it, kids, it's not like that. You'll be fine," he growled.

"But—"

The kids' distress whiplashed through the air. Jacqueline let her hand drop on Kenna's shoulder as the tears in the girl's eyes threatened to spill over.

"I'm sorry!" Kenna gasped. Her face twisted. "I wanted everything to go perfect and now…"

"Everything's still fine," Jacqueline reassured her, and Kenna's face pinched shut in a way Jacqueline knew too well.

She's not going to believe me that easy, Jacqueline thought. *And Tally's still screaming, and Dylan's on a knife's edge to start crying, too. How am I meant to fix this?*

Oh God. Arlo was right. I can't help them. I'm completely out of my depth. I don't belong here at all.

She met Arlo's eyes across the cabin. She wanted to yell "Help! Do something!" but what could he do?

Arlo climbed out from the bed nook. Standing straight, his head almost brushed the ceiling. "Kids," he began, and when that had no effect on the thunderstorm-heavy atmosphere: "Kenna, Dylan, Tally—"

Tally stopped screaming. The look of relief on Arlo's face was almost comical—and then he realized she'd only been sucking in another breath to scream even louder.

He ran his hands over his face and gave Jacqueline a look that was half-bashful, half-determined.

What's he doing? she wondered, and then watched amazed as he grimaced and shook himself. The shaking rippled down his body and he transformed into a huge black and gray wolf.

Kenna squeaked with surprise and transformed, flopping to the cabin floor as a spotted seal. Dylan changed shape, too, slipping awkwardly down the ladder. It was as though their transformations had caught them by surprise.

In Jacqueline's arms, Tally's kicking legs were suddenly kicking flippers. She wriggled through her sweater and Jacqueline kneeled to catch her before she hit the floor. She eased the tiny seal pup to the ground and bundled the abandoned sweater against her chest.

It was only when she started feeling light-headed that she remembered to start breathing again.

The three seal shifter siblings were gorgeous. They all had the same thick, glossy coats with mottled brown, gray and white coloration. And Arlo…

Jacqueline gulped. She was still kneeling down, and her eyes were level with Arlo's. He was a *wolf*, a *huge* wolf, with pointed ears and long legs tipped with heavy claws.

He should have looked like something out of a bad dream. The big bad wolf from a fairy tale. But…

Even in wolf form, his eyes were so… human. They were the same midnight-blue as before. But they weren't as closed-off and wary as his human eyes had been. His wolf's eyes practically overflowed with emotion.

Jacqueline's heart was in her throat. She felt as though the wolf-Arlo was trying to communicate something with her, but what?

He broke eye contact first. Jacqueline watched, frozen, as he sniffed at each of the seal pups in turn and barked softly. He shook his coat and flicked his ears towards the bed.

The seals *whined*. Jacqueline blinked. There wasn't any other word for it. Kenna made a grumbling noise that sounded so, so… *teenaged*. Even coming out of a seal's mouth.

Regardless of how much they grumbled and whined, all three seals followed what were obviously the wolf's instructions, and clambered up onto the bed. Tally was too small to make it by herself, so Arlo helped her, pushing his snout under her sausage-like body and boosting her up.

The kids cuddled together in a heap, their fat bodies making a cozy dent in the middle of the mattress. Jacqueline's breath caught as Arlo leaped up on the bed and trotted around them, gently pressing his nose to each of their snouts in turn. Tally gave a whuffly bark, and he licked her forehead. Then he picked up a corner of the blanket between his teeth, dragged it up over the seal pups, and lay down curled around them.

It was the strangest, sweetest picture of family love that Jacqueline could have imagined. And it hurt more than she could have imagined.

I have to get out of here.

She stood up so quickly her head spun.

"I, er," she muttered brokenly as Arlo raised his head and pinned her with those too-human eyes. "I just need to…"

Jacqueline gave a stupid smile and climbed, practically flew, up the stairs to the hatch. She wrenched it open and barely managed to stop herself from slamming the door shut behind her.

Up on deck, all her breath rushed out of her at once. She closed the hatch—slowly, carefully, not wanting to interrupt—made it to the side of the boat, and folded over the railing like a wet towel.

"What the heck was that about?" she asked herself when the world stopped spinning around her. As though she didn't know.

She stared out across the water for she didn't know how long. Darkness had properly fallen now, coating the world in inky black. The boat lights made rippling golden lines on the water. Far away, past the darker texture of black on the horizon that she assumed was the coastline, the sky glowed faintly.

Dunston, she thought. Home.

Her whole life was there, somewhere under that faint yellow glow.

And here on this boat, in the dark, gently rocking ocean…

"Jacqueline?"

CHAPTER EIGHT
Arlo

*J*acqueline wiped her eyes before she turned around. Arlo's chest clenched.

"Are you all right?"

Jacqueline smiled and shook her head slightly. "I'm fine."

Arlo frowned. His wolf was confused—the smile was an obvious lie. It didn't go to her eyes. It looked like it *hurt*, and that was wrong. His wolf wanted to go to her, to give her the same simple comfort it had offered the pups. They were asleep now, after all. And his mate needed him. Why wasn't he already at her side?

Humans are more complicated than that, he told it, and cleared his throat.

"You moved pretty quick back there, I was worried—"

"Are the kids okay? They got to sleep?" Jacqueline's voice teetered on the edge of brittle. Arlo took the hint.

"They're out like lights. It's—" he paused, and then added: "Things are simpler, when we're in our animal forms. Human worries don't seem so important. It's easier to let them go for a while."

Jacqueline's eyebrows pulled together. "That's good. But—what about their animal worries, are they—" She stopped, grimacing. "Sorry. This is none of my business. I shouldn't have—have forced you to bring me along."

You screwed it up. Now she thinks you hate her. Arlo's mouth was dry. He had to fix this. He'd panicked, before, but everything was under control now. The kids were going to Hideaway, and he could... try to make this work.

God, she was so—so—he bit back a groan. The sweater and pants she was wearing didn't cling to her body like her soaking wet dress had. What they did was a thousand times worse.

He knew what her body looked like. He knew what she *felt* like, those warm curves pressed against his side.

And now she was wrapped in *his* clothes. He knew that sweater like the back of his hand. Its fabric was softened by years of wear, but still warm and cozy. There were a few loose threads that he'd meant to darn but not gotten around to yet, because he only remembered them when they tickled.

As though the universe had heard his thoughts, Jacqueline wriggled slightly and slipped one hand under her—*his*—sweater. It was too easy to imagine his own hand sliding under the soft fabric to brush away the stray thread and resting, just for a moment, against her even softer skin...

She was gorgeous. Gorgeous and inquisitive and so brave.

His heart sank. She was perfect. She clearly had her life together. He'd have to be arrogant beyond belief to imagine there was any room for him in it.

He cleared his throat. "Is there anyone waiting for you back home? Like I said, I don't have a phone on the boat, but I can radio in and ask for a message to be sent through."

Jacqueline's face went carefully blank. "No," she said quietly. "I'd better call in to work about the kids' missing friend, and there's my work, but...

I don't think they're likely to check in on me until morning at the earliest. I'm free as a bird."

She didn't sound happy about it. Her hands were twisting together; no, Arlo saw as he looked closer, she was rubbing her ring finger. Her empty ring finger.

He'd thought he was an arrogant dick. Now he knew he was an asshole. Only an asshole would be as relieved as he was by something that clearly made her miserable.

"I'm sorry," he said. His voice was rougher than he'd intended, and he braced himself for her to flinch away, like people usually did when he started growling. It was all he deserved, after all. "I shouldn't have said anything."

"No, don't be." She didn't even seem to have noticed the roughness in his voice. She tucked her hands into the too-long sleeves of her sweater. "It's a sensible question. If there was anyone waiting up at home for me, I'm sure they'd be glad to know I wasn't lying dead in a ditch somewhere."

Her voice grated and Arlo was walking towards her before he could stop himself. He just managed to veer off at the last second and stand beside her, staring across the dark water towards the coastline, instead of wrapping his arms around her.

Jacqueline sighed and stopped rubbing her ring finger. "Not that it's really home anymore, anyway." She stared out over the water, her eyes squinting as though she was staring into the sun.

Before Arlo could say anything, she shook her head. "God, listen to me rabbiting on. You'd think I'd be happy to meet someone who doesn't already know everything about my life."

She glanced at Arlo nervously. He hoped his expression was reassuring. He wasn't a good judge of what other people thought of his face, for the most part.

"That must be one thing small towns all have in common, shifter or human," he said.

"Hah!" Jacqueline looked as though she was smiling despite herself. "We don't have telepathy, though. God. I can't even imagine how much worse that would be. Or maybe it would be better, maybe I would have—"

She took a deep breath and ran one hand over her eyes in a gesture that Arlo suspected was meant to look like she was pushing her hair off her forehead, not buying time as she got her feelings under control. "Forget it. I was meant to be somewhere else tonight, celebrating a, a fresh start. That's going to have to wait until the kids are safe."

Arlo's wolf whuffled its approval. Of course she was going to stay with the kids. And with him.

Arlo frowned. *We don't know that. We can't just assume everything's going to be all right. Not with*—he sighed. *Not with me involved.*

"You can always celebrate in Hideaway Cove," he suggested.

She actually smiled. Which he didn't understand, but hell, it was a win anyway.

"You know, that sounds even better than my original plan," she said. "What do you recommend?"

Dinner. With me. Here on the boat, under the stars, with all the time in the world to get to know each other.

Arlo swallowed. "There's a good restaurant in town—Caro's Hook and Sinker. Best chowder you'll ever eat."

"Celebrating a fresh start in Hideaway Cove. The town where people can turn into animals." Her voice echoed with wonder. "You're right, that does sound better than the Spring Fling, and being pawed at by the same guys who've been trying it on since I got single. Why did I ever think having a fresh start in my home town was a good idea?"

Longing flooded Arlo's veins, along with a protective anger at these men who'd bothered her. He should have said he would take her to Caro's. Invited her.

Or would she think he was as irritating as those men in her home town?

Jacqueline's eyes slid towards his and her cheeks went slightly pink. "I just want to be clear, what happened before, it's nothing to do with—well, what you can do. The wolf thing. Or the kids, of course."

Her cheeks went even more pink and she looked down at her hands.

"This is the first time you've ever met shifters." Arlo said. "You're taking it well."

"Have I ever met people who can turn into animals before? I think I'd remember that." Jacqueline shook her head. "But it's... I don't know. I feel like I *should* be more surprised than I am, but I'm not, and anyway the important thing here is making sure the kids are safe. So I'm not complaining. In fact..."

Her cheeks darkened again and she made a small strangled sound. Arlo jerked towards her, and just stopped himself from placing his hand over hers. "What?"

Jacqueline was still shaking her head. "I just figured out why I'm so fine with it all," she explained, laughing ruefully. "It's because you're all from Hideaway Cove."

Arlo sat back. "Hang on." He couldn't help the alarm bells going off in his head. "How so?"

"Don't worry." Jacqueline raised her hands. "No one in Dunston has a clue about shifters. Your secret's safe." She pushed a stray curl off her forehead and leaned against the railing again. "Hideaway Cove is our closest neighbor but no one really knows anyone from there. Which makes sense, since you're trying to keep yourselves secret. But it also means you're sort of like the creepy empty house at the end of the street that everyone says is haunted."

Arlo laughed. "Ghost stories?" *I'll have to tell Harrison. He'll be thrilled.*

Jacqueline grimaced. "More like you're the boogeyman to blame for everything that goes wrong. Silly stuff, like—oh, you know. The mail's late, must be Hideaway's fault! The wind's coming from Hideaway way, watch out for electrics playing up!"

"Wait." If he'd just heard what he thought—that was even better than ghost stories. "Electrics?" Arlo asked carefully.

"Oh, like… after this last storm. It came up the coast from Hideaway, and ever since then phone lines have been getting crossed, the mayor's electric car keeps doing wheelies down main street by itself…" Jacqueline trailed off. "What? You look like the cat who got the cream. I'm missing something. And—" Her expression changed, back to that almost-panicked wariness when she'd said she didn't belong here. With him. Arlo's chest tightened. "It's okay if it's a shifter thing, you don't have to tell me."

The more secrets you keep, the longer she'll feel like you're pushing her away. Arlo's stomach twisted. Is this what Harrison had felt, when he met Lainie?

"It is," he said out loud, "but mostly it's a work thing."

"Now I'm even more confused."

"I've been having a long argument with a friend of mine about… certain things. I'd like to be there when you tell him that story about the electric car doing wheelies."

Jacqueline raised her eyebrows. "He's going to lose a bet?"

"I'm going to win the I-told-you-so of the century." Arlo grinned.

"And…" Jacqueline licked her lips and Arlo's eyes tracked the movement. He met her gaze again to see it bright with curiosity and… excitement? Anticipation?

Damn it, he wasn't good enough at this. Telling people's feelings just from what they looked like. It was easy with the kids, but Jacqueline? She was a closed book.

He took a deep breath, but Jacqueline got in first.

"You're going to introduce me to this friend of yours?"

She still had that look in her eye. Arlo cleared his throat.

Please let this be the right answer. "Yes? There won't be any avoiding it, sorry. Hideaway Cove's pretty small. As soon as we dock, it'll be all questions."

Jacqueline was quiet for a moment. Her eyes searched his. Whatever she found there seemed to reassure her.

"Then maybe I'm meant to be here, after all," she said quietly.

Arlo's hand was less than six inches away from Jacqueline's. A shiver of wolfish anticipation went through him and he tightened his grip on the railing. Like he'd told her only a few minutes before, his wolf didn't understand human worries.

"I think you're exactly where you need to be," he murmured, his voice as gentle as he could manage. He wanted to say more, but his wolf was too bristling-high inside him, every nerve on edge, for him to make human words.

He stared pleadingly at Jacqueline and slowly, like the sun rising over still waters, her face lit up. Her smile was tentative, only half-believing, and God, he needed to say something, anything, to push that smile from a half-believing sunrise to full midday heat.

"Would you," he began, and stopped to clear his throat. "Would you like…"

CHAPTER NINE
Jacqueline

Jacqueline didn't breathe as she waited for Arlo to finish the sentence. Even her heart seemed to have stopped, as though her body didn't want to risk the thud of her pulse in her ears blocking out whatever he was about to say.

"...Dinner," he said eventually, and Jacqueline would have been disappointed if it wasn't for the sudden flash of regret in his eyes.

He hadn't meant to say dinner. At least, she thought not. Hoped not. God, she was practically dizzy. She wasn't even making sense inside her own head.

But—he said she was meant to be here. And that she was going to meet other people from Hideaway Cove. Those didn't sound like the words of someone who was going to tip her overboard the moment they were close enough to shore. They sounded like someone who wanted to spend time with her.

Oh lord, she thought, and swallowed down a sudden bubble of giggles.

He was still looking at her, an expression of mild panic in his eyes.

Something inside her melted.

"Dinner?" she said, and leaned the tiniest bit closer to him.

"The kids cleaned me out of fresh food, but…" Arlo shrugged tightly.

Was he nervous? How did a man who looked like that get nervous? Oh God. *She* should be nervous, but instead, she was edging closer to him, like he was some sort of giant mouse and she was a hungry cat.

"Cornbread isn't hard to throw together, and there's… tins of, uh… it's bachelor rations, but better than nothing. Since Tally ate most of your meal earlier."

Dinner. A shiver of anticipation went down Jacqueline's spine. She might be reading this whole thing wrong but until she had proof either way, couldn't she just enjoy pretending?

And if she wasn't reading Arlo wrong…

The shiver of anticipation turned into electric delight.

Jacqueline took a deep breath. "Dinner sounds lovely," she said.

"Right." Arlo's lips hooked into a bashful smile. "Good."

Jacqueline couldn't help smiling back.

Arlo crept below decks and returned with a box from the pantry. Jacqueline joined him next to the cooker.

"Can I help?"

"Sure. Could you oil the pan? It'll need a few minutes to warm up."

Jacqueline sat down beside Arlo and took the frying pan he handed her. They worked together in silence for a few minutes, Jacqueline lighting the cooker and Arlo mixing ingredients. By the time the pan was hot enough and the mix was ready, Jacqueline's mouth was watering.

Her stomach gurgled as Arlo tipped the dough in to cook. "Sorry. I'm starving, and that already smells delicious."

"Wait until you try it before you make any judgements. I'm only used to cooking for myself." Arlo fixed the lid on the skillet.

"The fish earlier was amazing. The bite of it I had, at least."

"You have to be a worse cook than me to ruin fresh fish and bread someone else baked," Arlo demurred. "This could burn, or not cook through, or…" He waved his hand as though encompassing a world of terrible cooking disasters.

"I see a fresh stick of butter in here," Jacqueline announced, digging in the box. "That's enough to fix anything, in my books." Her stomach growled again and Arlo gave her an apologetic look.

"I should have noticed Tally was staking a claim on your plate."

"I didn't want to stop her. God knows when those kids last had a hot meal."

"They won't have to worry about that anymore." There was a strange growly undertone to Arlo's voice. It wasn't threatening, though. If anything, it reminded Jacqueline of watching him curl around the kids downstairs. Warm and protective.

"It's amazing they've made it this far. Impressive, I should say. But I bet they're more than ready to stop being tough adventurers and just be kids again." Jacqueline's heart fluttered. "They're lucky you were nearby."

"They're lucky you were."

Jacqueline snorted. "What, so I could almost get myself drowned in front of them? Add some trauma to everything they've been through?"

"I would never have let that happen."

Jacqueline swallowed. The protective growl in Arlo's voice was so deep it rumbled in her bones, somehow grounding her and making her feel like she was flying all at once.

She met his eyes and let herself sink into them.

"I guess I'm lucky too, then," she breathed.

Arlo's gaze was warm and intense. The way he was looking at her, hopeful and bashful, pupils so dark they made the night seem bright… No one had looked at her like that in years. If ever.

"I'm the lucky one," he murmured.

He turned back to the pan. Jacqueline tucked her hands into her sleeves, even though she wasn't feeling the cold anymore. Her damp hair was

66

catching the breeze, but the warmth bubbling inside her swept away all the night's chill.

Maybe she would get her spring fling, after all.

CHAPTER TEN
Arlo

They will be safe here. Won't they?

Doubt had started prickling at the back of his neck when Jacqueline went to bed the night before and now, even the blazing mid-morning sun wasn't enough to burn it away.

There was no reason the three shifter children wouldn't be safe in Hideaway. The small town was a sanctuary for all shifters. They'd even taken Arlo in after he turned up in town, all snarled coat and teenaged surliness. Arlo wasn't sure even his closest friends, Harrison and Pol, knew how much the Sweets meant to him. Neither of their shifters were pack animals. Well, sure, maybe the Sweets weren't either—he didn't know how gators lived in the wild—but Ma and Pa Sweets had been better parents to him than his own pack had been after his mother's death, and now, assuming this Eric didn't show, they'd do the same for—

He shivered. *Why does that feel so wrong?*

"Cannonball!"

Dylan whooped and raced along the deck.

Don't— Arlo shouted, but it was too late. Dylan leaped off the side of the boat and landed in the water with a splash, his laughter echoing in Arlo's mind. Tally, who was sitting beside Arlo and "helping" him steer the rudder, chortled. *We're not anchored anymore. Don't make me turn this boat around!*

"He's okay!" Jacqueline called over from the bows. "Gosh, they're fast in the water, aren't they?"

There was a clatter as Dylan launched himself at the boat, shifted back into human shape midair, and scrambled aboard. "That was fun!" he gasped. "I'm going to do it again!"

His excitement fluttered against Arlo's mind and Arlo laughed despite himself. There was no point trying to reason the kid into behaving, that was for sure. After what the three of them had been through during the storm, this was probably the first chance Dylan had had to cut loose in ages.

Arlo decided to take a different tack.

"Don't you want to see Hideaway Cove when we come around the bluff?" he asked.

Dylan's eyebrows shot up. "Are we almost there?"

"You tell me. Can you sense we're close to other people like you?" The older shifters in Hideaway Cove kept their telepathic presences hidden, but the kids wouldn't be so careful, especially on a sunny weekend morning. The waves would be singing with excitement.

Dylan scrunched up his face. "Umm…"

Reach out like you're trying to talk to someone who's too far away for you to see, Arlo advised him.

Reach out? What do you mean? We're just talking.

Arlo laughed. *And that's why every other shifter around can hear you when you do. Don't think about it like you're just plain talking. Go look for someone to tap on the shoulder and whisper in their ear.*

Okay… Dylan screwed up his face until his eyes almost disappeared.

Um...

His telepathic voice faded out. He gasped.

You got it?

Dylan's eyes were shining. "There's heaps of people there!"

"Maybe a few hundred." Arlo leaned back and grinned, not hiding how pleased he was.

"A few hundred?" Kenna emerged from below decks, her eyes wide. She stared at Arlo in dismay and then looked out towards land. "And they're all waiting for us?"

"They don't know you're coming, yet," Arlo reassured her. Kenna had been below deck all morning, "getting ready". She'd been completely silent except for the occasional bolt of anxiety, but Jacqueline had reassured him that that was completely normal, and had loaned Kenna the contents of her handbag.

Her forehead wrinkled. "But—you told us yesterday we're really loud..." She bit her lip. *Dylan we've got to be careful, we don't want to be annoy—oh no...*

Kenna's face fell and Arlo held up his hands. "Don't worry. You won't annoy anyone. Day like this, half the kids will be on the beach, shouting about how much fun they're having to anyone in telepathic distance. You'll fit right in."

Kenna didn't look entirely reassured.

Jacqueline walked over and Arlo's wolf perked up. *She's—*

Yeah, yeah, I know. Happiness shivered across Arlo's skin as Jacqueline stepped down beside him.

He ran a careful eye over her. She didn't look any the worse for wear after her time in the water. Her eyes were bright, and her cheeks slightly flushed from the wind. Her red curls danced in the breeze.

"Morning, Kenna," she said. "Your hair looks nice. Did you find everything you needed in my bag?"

Kenna ducked her head and mumbled something. To Arlo's secret amusement, she mumbled telepathically at the same time. But her mind glowed with pleasure as she went to sit in the bows.

"We must be getting close," Jacqueline said, staring out towards the coast. "Is that a lighthouse?"

"Hideaway's just around that next bluff. Dylan, want to give me a hand guiding us in?"

Dylan's eyebrows almost shot off his face with excitement. He sat down beside Arlo and listened carefully as Arlo explained how to control the ship's direction.

Arlo's heart lightened as the *Hometide* slipped around the bluff and Hideaway Cove came into view. The small town sparkled like a jewel in the morning sun.

He glanced towards Jacqueline. Her eyes were shining, too, as bright as the calm waters around his home.

SWIM! cackled a voice in his mind, and movement flashed at the corner of his attention—Tally, making a bid for the freedom of the water. Arlo half-rose, but Jacqueline was already scooping her up.

"Hey now," she said, hoisting Tally in her arms so the girl could see the shore, "We'll get there faster on the boat than with you jumping overboard, okay?"

Tally's impatience batted against Arlo's mind, and his wolf huffed with amusement.

Jacqueline waited for Tally to respond out loud. When she didn't reply—but also didn't wail or shift into her seal pup form—Jacqueline raised her eyebrows at Arlo.

"I guess that's an 'okay'?"

His chest tightened so fast that his "Yes" came out more like a grunt. The light in Jacqueline's eyes, the smile dancing around her lips, even the way she'd smoothly out-maneuvered Tally's leap for freedom—it was almost too much.

I'm taking her home.

His heart thudded. *I'm taking her home. I should feel happy, not terrified.*

Dylan tugged on his arm. "What's that?"

Arlo followed Dylan's pointing finger. "That's the marina. I've got a berth along a bit further, by our workshop."

"No, what's *that*? And what workshop? And should I try to talk to him?"

"Where I work when I'm not out on the water." Arlo squinted across the water. If Dylan wasn't pointing at the marina, then what was he looking at?

Talk to him? What was he on about?

The water was calm past the entrance to the cove, with just a few ripples catching the sunlight. The water glinted gold where the light touched it, and—

Arlo groaned. It wasn't just the water glinting gold.

"You have got to be kidding me," Arlo muttered. Jacqueline shot him a questioning look and Kenna leaned forward, curiosity getting the better of her teenagerliness.

"What *is* that? It looks like—"

Damn it, Pol, this is not *the time,** Arlo growled to the figure shimmering through the water towards them.

What's not the time? his most irritating coworker replied. **You'd better be done sulking, because—wait, who are they? You've brought visitors? Why didn't you say?**

Arlo groaned. Jacqueline moved up beside him.

"Anything I should be worried about?" she whispered.

Arlo shook his head. "No, he's—" He broke off as Pol got closer and began to surface. **Damn it, Pol, you can't just—**

What? They're shifters, aren't they? I can hear them yelling in my head about what they think I am. Pol's psychic voice was irritatingly smug. **Smart kids you've got there.**

They're not mine, and it's not just them—

Before he could say "There's a human on board, too," Pol surfaced.

And stayed shifted, because of course he did.

Damned dragon, Arlo grumbled silently as the others gasped in amazement.

"No way." Kenna stood up, her mouth hanging open. "No *way*."

Dylan didn't say anything, but his eyes were wide as saucepans and he was so excited he was actually vibrating. Tally giggled and cooed happily, probably more from coasting the swell of her siblings' amazement than understanding how supernatural the sight in front of them was. And Jacqueline...

Arlo stopped himself from looking at her and glared at Pol instead. The last thing he wanted to see was Jacqueline speechless with wonder at the mythical beast that had burst through the waves in front of them.

Pol's dragon form was the length of a train car, slender and agile with gleaming scales and wings that looked like sails made from pure gold when they caught the light. When he was swimming, he kept them tucked close to his long, lizard-like body, so it was possible the kids just thought he was some sort of giant, malformed sea snake.

He glanced at their faces, lit up with wonder. Nope. No chance of that.

Pol poked his head out of the water as he dragon-paddled beside the boat. His neck was long enough that he could look onto deck and when he saw that Arlo wasn't alone, he did a dramatic double-take.

Well, hello! he said, broadcasting his voice to everyone on the *Hometide*. *Welcome to Hideaway Cove! My name's Apollo. What are your names?*

The kids replied—psychically and out loud.

Jacqueline swayed on her feet.

"They're... introducing themselves to the... dragon?" She took a small step closer to him and Arlo started finding it hard to breathe. "Am I supposed to as well?"

"Yes, he's a dragon, and right now he's being an asshole. Jacqueline, meet Pol. Pol—come up here and introduce yourself properly!"

He gritted his teeth. Pol was always annoying, but this was something else. Arlo didn't know why, but even his wolf was on edge as the dragon approached the *Hometide*.

Pol reared up and launched himself towards the boat. Arlo jumped up, grabbing Jacqueline around the waist to anchor her in place and calling to Kenna and Dylan to hold on.

Right, he thought, gritting his teeth. *This is why Pol turning up always gives me a sense of impending, exhausting doom.*

Pol managed to jump half-out of the water, landing with his front legs on the port side deck. The boat lurched to one side under his weight. Dylan hooted with laughter, Pol's claws scrabbled on the deck—Arlo was caught between irritation that he'd have to fix the wood, and satisfaction at seeing the dragon shifter less-than-graceful for once—and then there was a sparkle like goddamn fireworks and a moment later Pol was standing on the *Hometide's* deck.

Naked.

The younger kids didn't react; Kenna muttered "Gross" and went back to slouching over the bows.

"Wow," said Jacqueline, and Arlo's world froze solid.

Nope. His and his wolf's bad mood had nothing to do with Pol being a show-off, and everything to do with the fact that Pol was a shiny dragon shifter who looked like he stepped out of a movie screen, and Arlo still hadn't given Jacqueline any reason to think he was more than a salt-crusted sea hobo.

His gut twisted. If two shifters were mates, they knew immediately, bam, no questions asked and none needed. But when a shifter's mate was a human?

What if Jacqueline didn't feel the mate bond like he did? What if she didn't feel it at all?

What if she felt something for goddamned *Pol?*

"Wow," Jacqueline said again, and then, "O-kay."

She'd tipped her head back as though she was staring at the sky, but had her eyes closed, as though even looking away hadn't quite done the trick.

"You know, at first I thought maybe the kids were some sort of hippies, but I'm beginning to get the feeling that shifters have different feelings about clothes than the rest of us," she said to the sky.

"'Fraid so," Arlo replied gruffly. "Hey, Pol! Go find yourself some pants." He nodded sharply towards the cabin door.

To his relief, Jacqueline kept her eyes closed until the door clicked shut after Pol.

He glanced at her warily. She cracked one eye open and looked around until she met his gaze.

"Please tell me that's the weirdest thing I'm likely to see in Hideaway Cove," she whispered.

Arlo grimaced. *Let me count. Pol's the shiniest bastard in town, but then there's Harrison...* "Sorry."

Jacqueline groaned. "Then I hope you have a good bar in town, because I am going to need a stiff drink."

Arlo's heart leaped with hope. *That doesn't sound like a woman hopelessly in lust with a blond, godlike dragon shifter.*

He cleared his throat. "Anyway, that's Pol. He's another one who washed up in Hideaway a few years back."

"Washed up? So I don't need to worry about a whole family of dragons swimming over here after him?" Jacqueline asked faintly.

"Not—" Arlo began as the cabin door swung open.

"*Thankfully* not, is what he means to say," Pol announced, leaping through the door. He'd found some pants. Thank God. "I expect we'd have been driven out of town by now, if there was more than one of me. Arlo, what have you been up to? Who is this lovely woman?"

"Jacqueline March." Jacqueline held her hand out and Pol reached for it.
Mine! Arlo's wolf snarled. Pol's hand jerked back.

Did he hear that? Arlo was horrified. Usually shifters only heard their own animals. He'd never heard of someone's creature communicating psychically with another shifter, and certainly not when they were in human form.

Pol raised his eyebrows. *Everything all right, Arlo?*

Arlo desperately reined in his wolf, which was still snarling—*snarling!*—at how close Pol was. *Fine,* he muttered, and Pol's eyebrows shot up even further.

I see. His eyes slid sideways towards Jacqueline, who was looking at them both like they'd just gone mad, and Arlo's wolf raised its hackles. *That's how it is, is it?*

Arlo braced himself for Pol to say something embarrassing, but to his surprise, he simply withdrew his hand. Jacqueline made a short movement as though she was going to try to grab it to shake, which made Arlo's wolf whine.

Pol blinked, placed his hand on his chest, and bowed dramatically.

"My apologies. My name is Apollo Jenkins, but you can call me Pol."

"It's a pleasure to meet you." The faint hollowness was fading from Jacqueline's voice; Arlo's chest tightened as she visibly pulled herself together. "Arlo said you washed up here—does that mean you're a relative newcomer, too?"

"The most recent, not counting the prodigal daughter. Which I don't, personally. You don't count as a newcomer if you half-grew up in a place." He heaved a sigh. "I've been bracing myself to lose the crown, what with the new subdivision on the hill, but it looks like I'm going to have to hand it over earlier than expected."

He smiled at Tally, who promptly squealed with delight and shifted. Arlo dived forward to grab her before she wriggled out of Jacqueline's arms, and somehow he ended up with one hand on Jacqueline's waist, the other helping her hold Tally over one shoulder.

Pol's laughter echoed in his head. *I can't believe this. You sneaky bastard.*

"That's why I'm here," Jacqueline explained before Arlo could reply to Pol—or tell him to shut it. "These three—Kenna, Dylan, and Tally here—have been trying to make their way to Hideaway Cove. Arlo offered to bring them the rest of the way, and I…" Her cheeks glowed. "I, er, came along for the ride."

"You were traveling by yourselves?" Pol looked aghast. Kenna and Dylan had sloped up while the adults were talking, and at his words, Kenna scowled.

Pol exchanged an uncharacteristically serious look with Arlo and turned his attention back to Kenna. "Well you've fallen on your feet here, I'll tell you. Arlo Hammond might look like something he scraped off the bottom of his own boat, but—"

"I'm taking them to the Sweets. Until their actual guardian turns up." Arlo's chest twisted as he said the words, and that must have been why they came out as a half-growl. Three pairs of seal-shifter eyes snapped to his and the wave of disappointment crashing off the children almost made him rock backwards.

Arlo rubbed his temple as the emotions throbbed like the beginning of another headache. This was the right thing to do, he knew it—and what else could he do, anyway?

"I won't be far away," he reassured them. "No one will. Town's so small, everyone's in everyone else's pockets. Besides, the Sweets are my pack. Being with them is pretty much the same as staying with me, except you won't have to sleep on the floor of my workshop."

"I don't mind sleeping on the floor," Dylan said quietly. Arlo shook his head.

"Well, you don't have to," Arlo repeated. He smiled, but on the inside, his wolf was whining fretfully. Something about the situation was worrying it.

I don't have time to mull it over now, he thought. *Jacqueline and I have got to get these kids home.* His wolf calmed down a bit.

About that, Pol began, but was interrupted.

What about Eric? broadcast Dylan in a whisper that was probably meant just for Kenna.

Pol's eyes bulged. "There's another one?"

Jacqueline looked around the group. "Wait, did I just miss something again?"

A wave of guilt poured off Dylan. "We're talking about Eric," he explained. "We're going to find him, aren't we? He wants to live in Hideaway Cove too."

Arlo's stomach hollowed out. "Sure, kid," he said, trying to hide the surge of frustration that filled the suddenly empty space inside him.

This was what had his wolf so bothered. The kids needed help, and whoever this Eric guy was, their so-called uncle, he'd failed them. He didn't deserve to look after the pack—*kids*, he quickly corrected himself.

"I work at the council over in Dunston," Jacqueline said. "I can ask people there to keep an eye out and let him know where you are, if they see him."

"That covers the human side," Pol announced. "And Harrison will manage the shifter side. We'll round this Eric up before too long, you'll see. And then you can all play happy families in Hideaway." He shot Arlo a cheeky grin that he didn't even want to contemplate translating.

He had enough to worry him as it was. Once the kids were settled with Ma and Pa Sweets… maybe he and Jacqueline could go for that drink she'd mentioned.

CHAPTER ELEVEN
Jacqueline

A freaking dragon.

Jacqueline inspected Apollo—Pol—from under her eyelashes. In his human shape, dressed in a pair of Arlo's old pants—seriously, at this rate Arlo would be lucky if he had any clothes left—there was no sign that he was anything other than human.

But wasn't that the case with all of them? The kids just seemed like normal kids, if a bit strange—well, normal-for-kids strange. And Arlo…

Her heart fluttered as she glanced at him. He was showing Kenna and Dylan how to ease the boat into dock. The wind riffled through his hair and he looked up—to check their course, not to look at her, of course—but she blushed anyway.

"So, Jacqueline." Pol came over and leaned on the railing with her, though she noticed he kept a careful couple of feet of space between them. She blushed again, for a different reason. Everyone must have seen him avoiding shaking her hand earlier. Like she had cooties or something.

She suddenly realized she hadn't heard a word Pol had said. She shook her head.

"Sorry, what was that? I was distracted."

Pol chuckled. "Understandable! I was saying, so you're from Dunston? Did you get hit badly by the weather this last week?"

At least shifters are the same as regular humans in one respect. The weather is always a safe topic of conversation.

"Absolutely. The town's Spring festival starts this weekend, so everyone's glad things have cleared up."

"And you're missing the celebrations?"

"I was…" Jacqueline's brain swerved around the subject of *why* she hadn't been at the Spring Fling. "I work at the sheriff's office, and I was on phone duty last night. Not that that's usually much help to anyone after one of those storms…"

She told Pol about the urban legend of curses riding the breeze from Hideaway Cove. When she got to the bit about electronics going haywire, he went pale.

Oh God. Have I said something incredibly rude? What have I done now? She bit her lip.

"You're sure it was only after the storm?" Pol asked urgently.

"Ye-es." Jacqueline was still running over the last few minutes of conversation to make sure she hadn't accidentally said anything insulting. Joking about a tired urban legend wasn't insulting, was it? Or maybe it was for shifters. "I mean, it's probably just some crossed wires somewhere, or…"

"That wouldn't explain the car." Pol dropped his head into his hands and groaned. "I had no idea this was happening!"

His shoulders stiffened and he turned to Arlo. "Did you know about this?"

"Only since yesterday!" Arlo grinned. "Maybe it's time you got that electrician's certificate after all, eh sparky?"

"Haunted cars." Pol groaned. "This is humiliating."

"That's what makes it so great." Arlo's eyes sparkled mischievously as he caught Jacqueline's look of confusion. "If you hadn't guessed, Pol here is the friend I wanted to see hear that story. He's got some powers over electricity—some dragon thing that even he doesn't understand."

"Hey!" Pol objected.

Arlo snorted at him. "Half the places in town only run because he's poked his nose into them. I keep telling him he needs to learn how electricity is *meant* to work before he ends up wiring us all up backwards, but will he listen?"

"Haunted cars," Pol repeated.

Jacqueline laughed. She couldn't help it, it was too ridiculous. Pol looked so stricken, and Arlo so smug, and the kids were staring at the town like all of their dreams had come true.

Kenna and Dylan helped Arlo dock at the wharf next to his workshop. Pol, still looking vaguely shell-shocked, ducked inside muttering that he had to sort something out, and the remaining five of them headed for the main street.

"So you're telling me Pol just… magics up electricity for the town?" Jacqueline was still trying to get her head around it.

"Something like that, the idiot."

"What happens if he moves away?"

"That's why I call him an idiot." Arlo huffed out a breath and smiled. "Nah. He's an ass, but he's reliable. I doubt you'll have any more problems over in Dunston now he knows what was happening."

"Shame." Jacqueline caught Arlo's eye and grinned. "Watching the mayor chase after his car like it was a runaway dog was the highlight of my week. Until now, I mean."

"Now?" There was a strange light in Arlo's eyes.

"All of this." Jacqueline gestured to the street and the surrounding buildings.

Hideaway Cove looked like one of the touristy towns along the coast. The houses and shopfronts lining the main street were all old-fashioned, with painted shutters and carved curlicues on the eaves. It could have come straight off a postcard.

The main street—and it looked like there was only one—was wide, and a broad promenade stretched along its side, next to the water. Concrete steps led down to a sandy beach, and a small building partway down advertised ice cream.

Kenna and Dylan were walking slightly ahead of Jacqueline and Arlo.

81

Every few steps one of them would rush forward to look at something and then dart back and exchange excited whispers with the other. Tally was human shaped again and had been convinced to wear an oversized t-shirt like a dress. She kept running between them and Jacqueline and Arlo, laughing to herself.

"All of this," Jacqueline repeated. "And all of you. Seals. Wolves. Dragons. I don't think anything's going to top this."

"Arlo!"

A tall man with golden-brown hair strode up to them. Arlo waved him over.

"Harrison! Jacqueline, meet Harrison. Hideaway's mayor. Harrison, this is Jacqueline March."

"Pleasure." Harrison held out a hand and Jacqueline shook it. "My fiancée, Lainie—oh. Well, she's the one over there, on her phone."

Jacqueline looked past him to a short, blonde woman whose attention was locked onto her phone. As she watched, the woman sighed and put it away.

Harrison cocked an eyebrow at the kids. "And who are all of you?"

Jacqueline stood back as Arlo made the rest of the introductions. Harrison frowned as Arlo told him they were looking for the Sweets.

"Aren't they out of town this weekend? Lainie—" He called the woman over. "Didn't a little bird tell you the Sweets were away this weekend?"

"Jools said they were off at a bridge tournament or something," Lainie said.

"Playing against humans?" Harrison seemed surprised. "Ahh. *Winning* against humans. Securing Hideaway's safety from the human scourge by beating them at cards. Cunning."

"Feeding into their gossip networks, more like. How else are they meant to keep up with everyone else's secrets?"

"It's just a game," Arlo protested. "You're acting like it's some sort of secret warfare."

"To hear my coworker talk about it, bridge *is* secret warfare," Jacqueline said. "She spends most of the workday trying to plot how to beat this one other couple who keep taking out the pairs championships."

Lainie and Harrison exchanged a look.

"Maybe they're coming around, if they're happy to play against humans," Lainie suggested. "Slowly."

"Or maybe they're looking for fresh territory to chew on, now that people in Hideaway are starting to see through them." Harrison's voice was dry.

Jacqueline frowned. Everyone was keeping a light tone, but there was an undercurrent of something she couldn't quite get hold of going on under the conversation.

Lainie caught her eye and grimaced. "Anyway. If anyone's got a spy network, it's me. I think Jools sees herself as my personal James Bond. Letting me know when the coast is clear."

She put one hand over her midsection, and Harrison bent to kiss the top of her head.

"What do you want them for, anyway?" Harrison put an arm around Lainie's waist and pulled her close. It was an oddly protective gesture, given they were only talking about Arlo's foster parents, Jacqueline thought.

"The kids need somewhere to live until their pack leader gets here," Arlo replied. "The Sweets—"

"—have that going for them at least," Lainie said as Harrison's face darkened. He looked at her in surprise and she shrugged. "You kids are shifters, aren't you?"

Kenna and Dylan nodded. Tally joined in a moment later, copying her older siblings.

"Then I'm sure the Sweets would move heaven and earth to look after you," Lainie said dryly. "Regardless of what they think of the rest of us."

"Right." Something in Arlo's tone made Jacqueline look at him. There was a strange expression on his face. Discomforted and lost.

"Well, they're not here, anyway," Harrison said. He raised his eyebrows at the kids. "What do you want to do? We can put you up in the bed-and-breakfast—wait."

He frowned, and so did Arlo. Jacqueline connected the dots. Someone must have telepathically said something—and from the tense expressions on Kenna and Dylan's faces, it was one of them, and they hadn't meant to be heard.

"You know, this whole telepathy things seems like more trouble than it's worth," she joked, trying to break the tension. Lainie raised her eyebrows at her.

"No argument there," she said, and Jacqueline shot her a grateful smile for picking up the end of the tension-breaking stick. "I had to practically re-teach Harrison here to use a phone after we got together. Speaking of which, hon, don't you need to send out the red alert that another—dramatic gasp—*human* is walking the streets?" She winked at Jacqueline.

She must be human, too, Jacqueline thought.

Harrison shook his head. "I think the cat's out of the bag already, sweetheart. I might be wrong, but I do get the feeling this woman might already know about shifters. But that doesn't solve the problem of the Sweets not being here the one weekend they could make themselves useful."

"Hey," said Arlo in a warning tone. "They're still my parents."

"Sure, but you have to admit…"

"We could stay with you on the boat," Dylan blurted out, and Kenna punched him. "Hey!"

Arlo paused. "That's…"

His eyes slid sideways to meet Jacqueline's. For some reason her cheeks felt hot.

"Why don't you set up camp with us for the night," Harrison interjected. Lainie's eyes lit up.

"Yes! That's a great idea. We've got all these rooms no one is using."

Jacqueline expected Kenna, at least, to protest, but both children agreed. Tally nodded happily, too, and Arlo and Harrison winced in the way she'd come to recognize as evidence that the smallest shifter in their little group had the largest telepathic voice.

Lainie clapped her hands together. "Well, why waste time? We've got the Land Rover, so let's all trundle up the hill now and get you three settled in. And some lunch. I don't know about the rest of you but all this early morning strolling has left me starving."

"Up the hill?" Dylan asked, and Lainie gave him a conspiratorial wink.

"That's right. Didn't I say? We live next to the lighthouse."

CHAPTER TWELVE
Arlo

There wasn't room in the Land Rover for all of them; Arlo and Harrison decided to walk. Harrison didn't even wait for Lainie to start the engine before he started to interrogate Arlo.

So. Jacqueline.

Yes. Arlo gritted his teeth. *Did Pol tell you?*

Pol? I haven't seen him all day. I just have eyes in my head, is all.

Arlo groaned. *That obvious?*

You might as well be singing and dancing.

Arlo thrust his hands deep in his pockets and didn't reply.

Harrison frowned. *Why aren't you singing and dancing?*

Do I have to tell you?

She's human. It shouldn't matter. Harrison strode in front of Arlo and stopped, arms crossed. "It doesn't matter, does it?"

Arlo knew what he meant, and the knowledge tasted bitter. When Harrison first met his human mate, Lainie, Arlo had behaved like an ass. He'd fully bought the Sweets' line that Hideaway Cove could only be a sanctuary for shifters if they didn't let any humans settle there. He'd been afraid to lose the one place he'd been able to call home. And now?

Did he know better, now, or was he just afraid in a different way?

Doesn't matter anyway, he said. *Look at me. I'm not the sort of man a woman like that would want to date.*

"Huh! Is that what you think?" Harrison clapped him on the back and pulled his shirt off over his head. "Come on. A run'll clear your head."

He kicked his pants off and shifted. Harrison's griffin form was almost as magnificent as Pol's dragon, but the effect was slightly spoiled by him pecking around to pick up his discarded clothes.

Arlo shucked off his own clothes and shifted. His wolf stretched its legs, snapping its jaws as it shook off his human anxieties.

He nosed his clothes into a bundle and picked them up in his jaws.

Race you, Harrison laughed, and took off. His wings flashed in the sunlight and Arlo caught a swell of amazement from the Land Rover.

Flying's cheating! he called back. *Try running on those mismatched legs and see how far you get!*

By the time he got to the house at the top of the hill, Arlo was panting and, if not happy, then at least at some sort of equilibrium. He nosed through the front door and made his way to the guest shower.

"You need a change of clothes?" Harrison called from elsewhere in the house when he'd finished washing.

"These are—" *fine*, he'd about to say, then he actually looked at the clothes he'd brought up. His shirt was so faded even he couldn't remember what color it had once been, his pants had scuffs on the knees, and there were distinctly wolf-bite-shaped drool marks over everything. "Uh. Thanks."

"You know, you can't rely on a human to pick up on the mate bond straight away. You're going to have to rely on your good old-fashioned charm and good looks." Harrison tossed a bundle of clothes into the bathroom.

Arlo sighed. "That's what I'm worried about."

***

Showered, dressed, and full of dread, Arlo found Harrison on the deck outside. Harrison was laying out lunch on a picnic table overlooking the cove.

Arlo couldn't help but whistle. "This is just for lunch?"

"We do a lot of entertaining these days, what with me being the mayor and Lainie trying to steal allies off the Sweets," Harrison said frankly. "We count you among the already stolen, by the way."

"Sure." He wandered over to the table and reached for a bowl of brightly colored prawn crackers. An eagle-like screech stopped him.

"Sorry about that." Harrison cleared his throat. "Those are Lainie's. I won't kill you if you eat them, but she might. We have to order them in special."

"Message received." Arlo pulled his hand back as the Land Rover pulled up on the other side of the house. His wolf pricked its ears up. *She's here!*

Arlo smoothed down his shirt nervously and Harrison snorted at him. Footsteps clattered as the others entered the house.

"Showers are through there, lunch is—oh, God. Lunch. Harrison, can you show them around? I need to eat."

Lainie descended on the lunch table like a seagull who'd just discovered the world's biggest bowl of fries. She hugged the bowl of prawn crackers to her stomach and sat down with a sigh. "I should have invested in these instead of land..." She closed her eyes and popped a cracker in her mouth. "Mmm."

Arlo sat down awkwardly opposite her.

"How's that going?" he asked.

Lainie cracked an eye open. "Not fantastic," she said. "Are you *sure* there isn't a secret all-shifter newsletter for real estate?"

"Not that anyone's told me about," Arlo replied.

"Guh." Lainie groaned. "Well, we've sold enough sections and basic builds to make back our investment, at least. But I really want to branch out with shifter-y designs, you know? The architect I've got working on the subdivision has all these great ideas..."

Lainie had inherited half the hill they were sitting on from her grandparents, who'd settled in Hideaway decades ago. Since she moved to town, she and Harrison had been developing the land, adding more—and more modern—houses to Hideaway's stock.

Arlo frowned. "If you can't find enough shifters to move in," he began, and Lainie froze.

"You too?" she asked.

"I didn't mean—"

Lainie sighed and popped another prawn cracker in her mouth. "I'm not selling to humans. Shifter and shifter-adjacent only. You can tell Dorothy that. Should make her happy."

"I wasn't—"

"It's okay, Arlo. I know. You're in a tough situation." She waved his protestations away. "Let's just eat lunch, and I want to hear more about these kids you picked up out of nowhere."

Arlo sighed. Lainie was the best person he could talk to about Jacqueline—but he still didn't know her well enough to know how to make the conversational leap.

"They're amazing," he said instead. "I wish I was half as smart at their ages. They made it all the way here without being picked up by human authorities—but they don't have to do that anymore. Shifters look after their own."

Again, that little twinge of wrongness. Lainie's lip twisted.

"They sure do," she murmured blandly. "Lemonade?"

The door opened, and Arlo was already leaping to his feet before Jacqueline's voice floated out over the patio.

"Is this the right place?"

She was standing in the doorway. He opened his mouth to usher her to the lunch table, but no words came out.

Yesterday, soaked through and out of her depth, she'd been stunning. This morning, salty tangled hair and all, she'd been the most beautiful person he could imagine. But now?

Her hair shone in a mass of curls. Her eyes seemed brighter, somehow, and the soft t-shirt and jeans she was wearing caressed her figure.

Her cheeks went pink as she met his gaze, and then her eyes slipped past him to Lainie.

"Harrison lent me some of your clothes, I hope you don't mind," she said.

Lainie quickly reassured her, and then the others all appeared behind her. Jacqueline rode a tide of hungry shifters to the picnic table and ended up sitting beside Arlo.

"Dig in, everyone," Harrison announced, and for a few minutes there was nothing but the sound of happy eating.

Arlo felt Lainie's eyes on him. Even knowing he was being watched, he couldn't help stealing glances at Jacqueline. When she reached for the salt, he handed it to her. When her lemonade ran low, he refilled it before she'd even noticed she needed more.

Lainie narrowed her eyes.

"So what's the next step?" Harrison said once everyone had eaten their fill and was caught up on how three orphan shifters had turned up on their doorstep.

Kenna and Dylan exchanged a glance, and then:

We should tell them—

Shh! They'll hear!

Dylan winced, and Arlo wondered what it was that he'd been about to tell Kenna they needed to say.

Kenna was fiddling with the edge of her napkin. "We still don't know where Eric is," she said, and Jacqueline nodded.

"If I can borrow a phone, I'll call in at work and ask my boss to put the word out," she said.

"Go ahead. And I'll put the word out here. Someone might have heard something. If your friend does find his way here, we'll get you all back together ASAP," Harrison said.

"But apart from that…" Kenna tore little pieces off the napkin.

"Well, waiting around here doesn't sound like much fun," Lainie declared. "Why don't we all go back into town? If you're going to be staying here you might as well get to know your way around."

Arlo remembered Kenna's hesitancy about meeting new shifters earlier. "Or we can stay here. It's up to you."

"No! I mean, you don't need to hang around with us," Kenna said. "You and Ms. March can—um, I mean..."

"I'd like to see more of the town, too," Jacqueline said. "Er—if that's okay?"

"Why wouldn't it be?" Lainie stared hard at Arlo. "We'll just clean up here—"

"We'll help!" chimed in Kenna and Dylan. Tally cooed and waved her fork around.

There's something weird going on there, Arlo thought, watching them file through to the kitchen. *One minute they're upset because I can't put them all up in the* Hometide, *the next they're telling us not to wait around?*

He sighed and shook his head. The most likely explanation was "they're kids", with a chaser of "and they've been through a hell of a lot, so cut them some slack". But his wolf was worrying over them like a dog who'd lost its bone.

They just need some stability. And to be sure the rug isn't going to be ripped away from under their feet again. Ma and Pa Sweets will give them that, until Eric decides to show his face.

His neck prickled again. Somehow, that still felt wrong. And not just because he doubted this Eric fellow was ever going to show up.

He gathered up a handful of dishes and followed after the kids. Lainie waited until the kids had gone back to get another load, then cornered him.

"You and Jacqueline?" she asked. He'd have had to pretend to be an idiot not to get her meaning.

He nodded.

"And you haven't actually told her yet, of course." Lainie blew her bangs out of her face. "Be nice."

"I am nice!"

"Sure. I know that. But it takes a while to get past the crusty exterior to your nice squishy insides." She folded her arms. "I'm serious, Arlo. It's better now than when I first got here, but I won't lie, it's hard. Hideaway Cove is a sanctuary but if you're her mate then your job is to be *her* sanctuary. And you're a bit too close to the sharks for that to be easy."

Arlo's heart sank. "You mean the alligators." Dorothy and Alan Sweets were alligator shifters.

"Bingo."

Kenna and Dylan came back in then and Arlo slipped out while Lainie was distracted.

Jacqueline called her office, and by the sound of it only managed to talk to the answering machine. She shrugged when Arlo gave her a questioning look.

"Either they'll check it or they won't. And frankly, if they end up thinking I've drowned myself because they forgot to check the freaking answering machine, it's no skin off my nose." She reassured Kenna and Dylan, "I made sure to ask about your uncle Eric. If they check the message, they'll know to send him this way if anyone sees him."

"And I've put the word out around my contacts out of town," Harrison added. "Now, who's ready for ice cream?"

Tally was almost snoozing by the time they started down the hill again. They all walked this time, after a short argument where Lainie reasoned with Harrison that, even if she was too tired to walk back up later, he could always carry her.

Arlo watched them bicker companionably.

They've been together for—what, six months?

Arlo counted back. Lainie had first arrived in town the previous autumn, and one winter of bad storms had cemented their bond. Arlo couldn't imagine either of them without the other now. Lainie might not be a shifter, but she was as much a part of Hideaway Cove as any of them, even if some locals—mainly the Sweets, he thought with a pang—still didn't totally accept her.

Six months, and the rest of Harrison's life stretched out in front of him, shining like the sun on still waters. Marriage. A baby. Maybe not in that order, depending on how quickly they managed to organize the wedding.

And Arlo...

Jacqueline was walking a little ahead, with Tally bundled sleepily over her shoulder. Lainie was walking with her.

"So, how long will you be in town, Jacqueline?" Lainie asked.

"Honestly? I wish I could stay forever." Jacqueline laughed, but softly, as though she was trying not to disturb Tally. "But I have work, and a house back in Dunston... Now that the kids are safely here, I should probably be heading back."

Arlo swallowed, and Lainie shot him an entirely too innocent look.

Arlo had less than a day, if he was going to have even a chance at six months, or longer.

They reached the promenade, the wide pedestrian area that stretched the length of the main street on the water side.

"Ice cream! Ice cream!" Dylan yelled, running towards the small shop halfway down the promenade. The sign, Sweet Dreams Ice Cream Parlor, used to make Arlo's stomach rumble just looking at it.

Arlo groaned. He wouldn't have minded going there earlier, but they'd run into Harrison and Lainie and bypassed it. Now, after what Lainie had said about his foster parents...

"Can we?" Dylan begged Kenna, who bit her lip.

"Eric has all our cash..."

Arlo straightened his shoulders. The parlor belonged to Tess Sweets, his foster parents' granddaughter. "My treat. Come on."

CHAPTER THIRTEEN
Jacqueline

Jacqueline didn't miss the way Arlo straightened his shoulders just outside the ice cream parlor door. Almost as though he was preparing himself for battle.

He stepped through—and then backed out as though a swarm of bees was after him.

Jacqueline caught his arm. He was wincing and clutching his head. "Are you okay? What happened?"

"Loud," he grunted, and Jacqueline looked past him to see the ice cream parlor full of... kids?

Dylan shrieked with excitement and ran in to join the throng.

"Ah." Jacqueline nodded and let the door swing shut. Arlo was still clutching his head, so she guided him carefully away, towards a seat overlooking the water. "A thousand happy screams, direct to the inside of your skull?"

"Yeah."

"Do you need some space?" Which she one hundred percent wasn't giving him right now, clinging to his arm like this. If he insisted, though...

"It'll pass." One side of his mouth hooked up. "Or I'll get used to it."

He didn't pull away from her, so she didn't let go. Her hand fit into the crook of his elbow like it was meant to be there.

"Headache?" Harrison dodged past them en route to the ice cream shop. The door swung open and Arlo winced again. Harrison looked bemused. "The kids? I know you've always been more sensitive to it than me, but— geez, Arlo. Are you all right?"

Arlo scowled at him and must have said something telepathically, because Harrison shrugged his shoulders and backed off.

"I'll grab you a cone," he said. "Caramel, right? What about you, Jacqueline?"

"Caramel sounds great."

"On it."

Arlo sighed heavily as Harrison went inside, and sat down on the seat. Jacqueline sat next to him. They weren't as close as they had been on the rowboat, not hip-to-hip... but close enough, with her hand still folded under his arm.

"Part of me is glad that didn't work," Arlo admitted ruefully. "Saved by the screams of a hundred happy children."

"There can't have been more than five people in there," Jacqueline protested.

"And Tally. She counts for at least fifty by herself." Arlo smiled, then his expression became serious. "My sister owns the ice cream parlor. With the kids, and my parents... maybe it's best I don't see her right now."

"But I thought your parents were going to look after them?"

"I..." Arlo raised his hands and dropped them in defeat. "I need to figure some stuff out." He frowned.

"Like how you're the only one who get migraines around the kids?" Jacqueline bit her lip. She still wasn't sure whether she should mention all these things she was noticing. She was probably reading things wrong, and even if she wasn't... she was only going to be here for a day. It was none of her business.

Arlo smiled weakly. "That. And some other things." He hesitated, and then wrapped his hand over hers. "I was wondering..."

Warmth spread across Jacqueline's skin. "Oh."

Arlo tensed. "Good oh, or bad oh?"

Jacqueline laughed out loud. Here she'd been, tying herself into knots over missing out on her spring fling, and Arlo was practically throwing himself in her lap. At least, as close to throwing himself as she imagined the quiet, stoic man ever got.

"Good oh," she reassured him. "Definitely. What were you wondering?"

"That, for a start." He looked down at their intertwined hands.

"Do you have your answer?" Jacqueline's skin was humming. God, this was incredible. She was just holding hands and felt like she was flying. She was sure it hadn't been like this with Derek, even at the start. Why had she waited so long to stop being a sad lump at home and get out and enjoy her new life as a single woman?

"I hope so." He cleared his throat. "I know you wanted to stay until the kids were settled in. With the Sweets not being here yet…"

"With what not what? Who are we talking about?"

"Dylan!" Kenna's groan was like a jet engine dying.

Dylan torpedoed around the seat, and Jacqueline had to whip her head back to avoid getting an ice cream cone to the face.

"With, er… is that for me? Thanks." Jacqueline inspected the ice cream carefully. "Caramel?"

Kenna slouched into view. "Apparently. The lady said she experiments with the flavors."

"Is that why it's green?"

Kenna handed Arlo his cone and Arlo gave it a suspicious look. "Tessa," he sighed, and then: "Cheers."

He bumped his cone against Jacqueline's.

It tasted like…

"Sort of caramel-y… seaweed?"

Dylan burst out laughing. "Yes! That's what it said on the board!"

"Seaweed caramel." Arlo shrugged and took another bite. "I swear, Tessa is wasted in this town."

"Tessa is your sister?" Jacqueline licked the cone again. It was strange, but it was kind of growing on her.

"Tess, I mean. That's what she prefers now, anyway, even if I keep forgetting." Arlo licked his ice cream again and frowned. "She's my foster parents' granddaughter. I guess technically that makes her my foster niece, but she says that makes her feel like she should be nine years old, so, sister it is."

"She said she wanted to talk to you," Kenna said. "She just needed to finish serving—oh, there she is."

Arlo's fingers tightened around Jacqueline's. She turned to look where Kenna was pointing, and caught a glimpse of a strange expression on Arlo's face. Almost as though he was scared.

When she glanced at him again, the expression was gone, so quickly she must have imagined it was there in the first place.

The woman walking over from the ice cream parlor looked a few years younger than Jacqueline. She had her hair pulled back under a retro-style hairnet, and huge dark eyes behind thick-framed glasses.

When she spotted Jacqueline and Arlo sitting together, those huge eyes got even bigger, and she spun around and darted back into the ice cream parlor.

"What—" Arlo began, and frowned. "One moment," he muttered to Jacqueline, and his eyes went vague.

"He's mindspeaking to her," Dylan explained.

Jacqueline raised her eyebrows. "Oh. You can hear?"

"No, because he's *really* good at it." Dylan heaved a sigh. "But it feels kind of buzzy against my brain. It's nice."

"How's your ice cream?" Jacqueline didn't want to guess at what flavor Dylan's bright pink cone was.

"Really good!" his eyes lit up. "It's like cotton candy."

"I got chocolate," Kenna said, ducking her head. "Not chocolate-and-anything, just chocolate."

"And what did—wait, where's Tally?" Jacqueline stood up. *Oh God. I lost one of them.*

Arlo snapped to attention. "What is it?"

"Tally's—"

"With Ms. Eaves and Mr. Galway," Kenna said quickly.

Who? Jacqueline thought. Arlo caught her confused look.

"Lainie and Harrison," he explained.

"Oh. Good." Jacqueline sat down. Her heart was racing, and everyone was staring at her. "I guess I'm more on edge after what happened yesterday than I thought."

Dylan was jumping on his heels and tugged at Kenna's sleeve. "Yeah, I *know*," she muttered, shaking him off. Despite her surly tone, her face was glowing.

Jacqueline sat back. Her ice cream was melting, so she ate a few bites while she gathered her thoughts.

Arlo still had that second question for her. And she had a pretty good idea what it might be.

She'd let go of his hand when she stood up, but even the memory of his fingers wrapped around hers made her skin go hot all over.

She knew what she wanted that second question to be and, damn it, she knew where she wanted the answer to land her. Not on a car back to Dunston that evening, that was for sure.

There was still one more day left to the weekend.

"I was saying that I've decided to stick around for the rest of the weekend," she said, and Arlo made a soft, strangled noise that made the heat on her skin blaze. "At least to see you kids settled."

And spend more time with the hot guy who saved my life, she added privately.

98

CHAPTER FOURTEEN
Arlo

*H*arrison appeared a few moments later, surrounded by small children and with Tally on his shoulders and half of her ice cream running down the side of his head. He rounded up Kenna and Dylan and led the shrieking mob straight into the water.

Arlo watched them, his head still spinning. One minute he'd barely as good as hinted to Jacqueline that he'd like her to stick around—and the next she announced she was staying the night.

His wolf growled happily and he shushed it. *In town. Not with me. That's not...*

He shook his tangled thoughts away.

Jacqueline was watching the water, too, her face glowing.

"So, what was your second question?" she asked chirpily.

Arlo stiffened. "My—? Oh." His tongue felt thick. "I, er." Her hand was warm in his, small and soft but strong, too. "I was wondering if you'd like to join me for dinner."

Jacqueline's lips twitched, as though she was trying not to let a smile escape. "I'd like that. Very much. Dinner and a drink," she declared, "to make up for your shiny friend earlier."

Arlo's head was ringing. "Yes," he said, and tripped over his tongue again. "That sounds, yes. I'd like that."

"Before then…" Jacqueline seemed lit up from inside. "I'd love to know more about Hideaway Cove. Would that be okay? Since Harrison said the cat's out of the bag already…"

She wants to find out more about Hideaway. She wants me *to show her my town.*

"Of course," Arlo said. "Where do you want to go first?"

They sat and finished their ice creams, watching the kids play in the surf. Other Hideaway locals joined them and Arlo pointed them out—including the seagull sisters Jools and Jess, who soared over in their gull forms and then, when they saw the newcomers, flew off to get changed and dressed and raced back to the beach.

"I don't know if you saw the Rodríguez kids before." Arlo pointed to three dark shapes flitting through the water out past the breakers. "Diego, Aarón and their baby sister, Ana."

"A friend for Tally?"

"She's closer to Dylan's age. I think." Arlo frowned. "Never been good with kids' ages."

"I'm not sure how old Tally is. Not older than three, though, I think." Jacqueline sighed. "Those kids have had a rough few years. I'm glad they're here now."

She sounded sad—but determined, too. Then she sighed. "I'd like to say I'll stick around until I'm sure they're settled, but… work…" Her voice dropped. "You know, yesterday morning, I was half planning to quit?"

Arlo's heart leaped. "Why?"

If she didn't have her job keeping her in Dunston—he cut the thought off before it could overtake him.

Jacqueline shrugged. "I feel like I've been… stuck, these last few years.

I've finally gotten rid of the last thing that's been holding me back, and I was ready to let everything else go, too. Except now, seeing the kids like this… knowing how quickly everything can fall apart… except I already *know* everything can fall apart…"

She shook her head, glared at the remains of her ice cream cone, and ate it in two bites. "Sorry. I'm not making sense. How about that town tour you mentioned?"

"Sure." Arlo stood up. "Let's start…"

His mouth went dry. *Let's start by introducing her to shifters whose first thought will be to realize she's my mate. And whose second thought will be…*

What the hell is the Sweets' boy doing with a human?

He gulped.

"What about your workshop?" Jacqueline suggested, and Arlo let out a huff of relief.

"Great idea."

***

"You still here, Pol?" Arlo pushed the workshop door open and ushered Jacqueline in before him. "Pol?"

The foyer was small. There was a low sofa against one wall, which Pol usually spent the working day lounging in, and a desk with an old computer and half-alive potted plant on it. The room was a bit dusty, a bit worn—but with Jacqueline in it, it lit up.

There was a strangled noise from further inside. Arlo raised his eyebrows and exchanged a look with Jacqueline. She snorted and covered her mouth.

"It feels like we're sneaking in," she whispered, tiptoeing into the foyer. "So this is where you work?"

"When I'm not on the water. The three of us—Harrison, Pol and me—went in on this place together a few years back."

"Isn't Harrison the mayor?"

"And our builder and handyman. Pol looks after electronics—well, you already know how well that goes—and I do boats. And other carpentry. It's not guaranteed work, but with the number of boats around here and the sea doing its best to beat the town underwater, it's as close as you'll get."

"So you work on buildings all around town? If I go out and look, I'll be looking at places you had a hand in making?"

"Or at least maintaining."

"That's wonderful." Her gaze went distant. "It must be great, knowing the work you do is so important to the town."

"Don't you work at the sheriff's office?"

"The sheriff's office in Dunston," she said, as though that said everything. She caught the expression on his face and waved her hands. "I worked as a tutor during high school, to save for college. Then after I got married I got the job at the sheriff's office, and... kind of kept up the tutoring?" Arlo must have still looked confused. "Dunston is a quiet town. There *is* a lockup at the sheriff's office, but mostly Reg just uses it to hold any teenagers he finds getting drunk or frisky where they shouldn't. And they tended not to have done their homework before they went out to get into trouble, so... I guess I'm still tutoring. Still doing the same high-school job anyone could do, and not particularly contributing to anything else."

Arlo frowned. "I bet the kids you taught would say different."

"I'm not a teacher. It's just... homework help. While they try not to vomit into buckets." She sighed. "Never finished that degree, after all. Anyway. We were talking about you. You like the boats best?"

"Of course." He wanted to ask her more about herself, but she'd made it clear that she'd prefer not to. And she seemed interested in his work, so he added: "I built the *Hometide* myself."

"No!"

"It took me the best part of five years." He led her through to the main workshop. The air was filled with the scents of wood dust and oil. Arlo breathed in deep. It smelled of long days of hard work.

Jacqueline grimaced. "I just spent the best part of five years... never mind. Is this for the boat?"

She walked over to Arlo's bench and, when he gestured it was okay, picked up a wooden frame.

"How did you guess?" *How* did *she guess?*

"It's the same size as the broken window above—" Her cheeks went pink. "Above, um, the bed."

"I'm trying to decide what to put in it." Arlo tried to keep the growl out of his voice, but his wolf was very interested by the way Jacqueline was blushing. "Plain glass, or..."

He stood next to her in front of the desk. She was so close he could smell her feminine scent under the wood, oil and smoke of the workshop.

Before the crowbar headache had hit him, he'd planned to spend the down-time after the house build working on a leadlight for the boat's bedroom window.

"I've been collecting these pieces of colored glass for a while," he said, sorting through a cardboard box of offcuts. "Watched a few videos online about how to do it. We've got all the tools here, I just need to decide what to make."

"You just watched a few videos and you can jump straight into making something?" Jacqueline sounded amazed. "You're not worried you'll ruin it?"

"If it goes wrong, I can always have another go. There's enough glass in here for a couple of bad tries."

"But what if..." Jacqueline twisted her hands together. "What if it goes wrong every time? Or there's one... design... that you really want to work, but it doesn't, and you can't try it again? Or... or maybe it's the first time you're having a go at it in a long, *long* time, and you don't want to mess it up?" Her cheeks blazed.

Arlo gazed at her, lost for words. He'd always been extra sensitive to other shifters' psychic signatures. He could feel emotions before he could see them, most of the time. Maybe that was why the kids had given him such a headache.

He'd never been good with humans, because he didn't have that cheat-sheet emotional background when he was talking with them.

But even an idiot like him could tell Jacqueline probably wasn't talking about stained glass windows anymore.

"It can be scary, trying something you haven't done in a long time... or ever," Arlo said carefully. "But I know that if something's meant to work out, it will." He paused. "And... I'm good with my hands."

Jacqueline blushed even harder. Her eyes flicked up to meet his. They were bright hazel, like intricately patterned heartwood, and the longer she kept his gaze, the warmer and more intense they became.

Something you haven't done ever. The words shivered down his back.

Arlo licked his lips. "Jacqueline," he said, her name like a prayer, "there's something I should tell you. Something about shifters."

"What is it?" Jacqueline's eyes filled his vision.

"I..."

"Aargh!" A heartfelt groan split the air.

Arlo jumped in front of Jacqueline. "Who—damn it, Pol!"

Pol was slumped in the door. He didn't even look up as Arlo swore at him. He was holding a battery in one hand and a lightbulb in the other, connected by wires.

"How does it *work?*" he groaned, hopelessly banging the two together. "It makes no sense!"

"Oh God," Jacqueline breathed from behind Arlo. "That's your friend with the electric powers. Did I break him?"

Arlo looked over his shoulder. Jacqueline looked stricken, but when she met his eyes, she stuffed her hand into her mouth to stop herself laughing out loud.

"Pol, read a book," Arlo told Pol as the dragon shifter slid down the doorframe in despair. "Jacqueline, I had a thought. Want to take the scenic route to the restaurant?"

***

This is safer than parading her in front of all my parents' neighbors, Arlo thought as they climbed the hill behind the workshop.

"This is like a goat path," Jacqueline said, panting slightly. "Or a..." She glanced at him and bit her lower lip.

"Wolf path?" Arlo suggested. He grinned. "If the weather's too bad for sailing, I'll come up here. Watching the water is almost as good as being on it."

Jacqueline put her hands on her hips and gazed out over the bay. The sea breeze tugged at her curls. "You come up here when the weather's bad?"

Arlo sighed. "Pol calls it my sulking perch."

Jacqueline laughed. "No!" Her grin turned wicked. "There's no way you could *perch* up here when it's windy. You'd need to cling on..."

"To this shrub," Arlo agreed, pointing at a nearby tree, twisted by the elements.

Jacqueline laughed again and the wind teased a hank of hair over her face. She pushed it back, giggling. "I guess this is the next best thing to being out on the water. It must be amazing, watching a storm from up here."

"That it is." He sat down and she settled in next to him, close enough that their arms brushed together and it seemed like the most natural thing in the world to take her hand. "I don't know why it is, but the sea always makes me feel at home. Tess says I should have been a fish shifter."

"Or a seal?"

Something jolted in Arlo's heart. "Or a seal," he repeated, slowly.

"I can't believe that Hideaway Cove exists, that you all live here openly as shifters, and none of us knew anything about it." Jacqueline gazed out over the water.

"Except about the curse?" Arlo joked, and was rewarded with an

105

embarrassed smile.

"Except the curse, yeah." She sighed. "I've lived in Dunston all my life. I knew there was a whole big wonderful world out there, I just didn't know *how* wonderful. Or how close it was. I've spent all my life around people who know exactly who I am and what my story is, and all along..."

She hesitated. Arlo stayed silent, unable to take his eyes off her as the smile faded from her face.

"You must have all sorts of strategies in place to keep the fact that you're shifters secret from visitors, I'm sure. But when I think I could have driven a few hours out of town and been in a place where no one knew my husband left me five years ago, and no one's gonna corner me in the grocery store and tell me how his kid's in second grade now... I'm sure you all would have done your best to drive me out of town, but even that would have been a step up."

Arlo put one arm around her and she leaned into him.

"Sorry," she muttered. "You brought me up here for a romantic walk and here I am, grouching about my ex."

"It's the sea." Jacqueline stared at him, eyebrows furrowed, and he gestured out over the water. "That's why I come up here. And why I go out on the water. I know that whatever bad thing I'm feeling, the sea will pull it out of me."

Jacqueline took another deep breath, and under Arlo's arm, her shoulders relaxed.

"I think it's working," she said quietly. "I do feel better. Better than I have in a long time."

Arlo wasn't good at picking expressions, but even he could hear the weight behind her words. He frowned.

"You broke up with your husband five years ago, but he has a kid in second grade?"

Jacqueline groaned. "Damn it. I hoped you wouldn't pick that up."

"I shouldn't have mentioned it."

"No, it's fine." Jacqueline let her head rest against his shoulder. "That's why we split. This other woman, she gave him what he'd always wanted, which I... anyway. He got what he wanted, and I got the house, which I've just paid off. Next stop, Vegas!"

There was a hard edge to her voice, despite her toothy smile.

"Well I'm glad you've stopped by Hideaway Cove on your way to Vegas," Arlo said, his voice gravelly. Jacqueline's eyes flicked up to his.

"Me, too," she said. "Though I think I've had enough sea therapy for one night."

"In that case," Arlo said, helping her up, "I think it's time we had that drink."

He showed her the back route to Caro's restaurant, picking their way through low shrub along a path that existed mainly in the mental maps each citizen of Hideaway had of the land around their town.

He pointed out the ridge where Jools and Jess had dared each other into leaping from to learn to fly, the small cave where local kids invariably ended up when they were skiving off from the town's correspondence school classes, and the wild herbs Tess had used for her experimental ice cream flavors before she graduated to seaweed. All the small and secret places that hinted at the heart of the small town he called home.

By the time they clambered around to the path that led down to Caro's, Jacqueline's cheeks were red with exertion. Arlo took her hand to steady her as she jumped across a muddy creek. Her hand's warmth, and the way she puffed slightly as she blew a stray curl out of her eyes, made him want to smack himself. He cursed underneath his breath.

"Sorry," he said when Jacqueline raised her eyebrows at him. Even he could tell that was a questioning look. He hunched his shoulders. "It's just struck me that this might not have been what you meant when you said you wanted a tour of the town."

"What?" Jacqueline blew her hair out of her face again. "Are you kidding? The sea therapy I could probably have done without, but this? I haven't done anything like this since I was a kid."

She frowned as her hair bounced over her face again, and let go of his hand to grab it and braid it into a long rope.

"Which must be obvious, since I've apparently forgotten what the wind is like this close to the water," she added, sticking the end of the braid under her collar. "I hope this restaurant isn't too fancy. I bet I look like a mess."

Arlo swallowed. With her hair pulled back, Jacqueline's eyes seemed bigger and more full of light than ever.

"You're fine," he said gruffly. "Caro's isn't a shirt and shoes place. People eat there straight after coming off boats, or work sites, so you'll—I mean, shit, not that you look like you've—you look lovely. You…"

Tell her. The words thudded in his bones. *Look how she already seems to belong here. The wind in her hair and light in her eyes. She's the piece of your heart that's been missing all these years. Tell her you're hers, tell her she's part of your pack—*

Take her to meet Ma and Pa. Arlo's mind tripped over itself.

"…You're beautiful," he said instead, and the dazed delight in Jacqueline's eyes almost made his cowardice worth it.

"Well." Jacqueline folded her lips over a smile that looked like it was threatening to take over her whole face. "You know, you're not bad yourself." Her cheeks blazed as she tucked her arm into his.

It can't be this easy, Arlo thought as she smiled up at him. *And yet…*

Maybe it could be. A shifter's mate was meant to be the other half of their soul; why was he surprised that Jacqueline was slipping so easily and wonderfully into his life?

She doesn't know what she is to me, but she's taking a chance on me anyway. Arlo swallowed. *After almost drowning, babysitting three frightened shifter kids, and having to put up with me grumbling and growling all the time. Sure, she's taking a chance on me now, for one date, but I need to do better than this before I tell her.*

The path took them to the back of Caro's restaurant; Arlo led Jacqueline around piles of neatly stacked pallets and other delivery detritus, silently cursing himself for not thinking this plan through properly.

"Are you sure it's okay for us to be back here?" Jacqueline asked, picking her way around a stack of insulated buckets. Arlo recognized them from the Menzies' fishing boat.

"Sure," he said, biting the inside of his cheek. *Great job,* he snarled to himself. *Sneaking around the back with all the trash. Are you* trying *to put her off?*

His stomach twisted, but before he could berate himself any more, a door swung open in front of them.

"—out of the oven, and the chocs from Tess's are—what's this?"

Caro loomed in the door. She was in her late forties, with short-cropped brown hair and a deep scar running along one cheek. In Arlo's eyes she was the backbone of the Hideaway community. Forget Harrison and his mayor's chain, and the Sweets with their bridge-and-gossip group picking over the latest news: there wasn't a person in Hideaway who hadn't eaten to bursting in her restaurant, and dozed off their delicious gluttony in front of her blazing fireplace.

"Oh!" Jacqueline's hand flew over her mouth. "I'm sorry, we were just— we were, um—" She dissolved into giggles. "Oh, God, this is *just* like sneaking around as a teenager. I swear, if someone threatens to call my Mom…"

"It's me," Arlo called, putting one hand on Jacqueline's shoulder as he sent Caro a jumbled telepathic explanation: *This is Jacqueline—human— visiting from the next town over—shifter kids—pack—dinner?*

She frowned at him, which was no surprise given the pack of nonsense he'd just vomited at her, then shook her head. "I'm Caro," she said, holding out a floury hand. "Nice to meet you…"

109

"Jacqueline." Jacqueline shook Caro's hand, either not noticing or not caring that it was covered in flour.

Caro's eyes flicked to Arlo's. *She's human?*

She's...

Ah. Caro's jaw set and then she shrugged. *Figures.*

Arlo's stomach stopped twisting. If Caro was happy to welcome in a human with no connection to Hideaway Cove, then maybe...

Caro jerked her head over her shoulder. "Come on in." She snaked a grin at Arlo that made her scar pull. "Your usual spot's free, but I'm guessing you might be after a table tonight?"

Damn it, Caro, Arlo growled. *I'm trying to...*

His telepathic voice faded away. What was he trying to do? Put his best foot forward? Prove to Jacqueline there was more to him than just growliness and terrible ideas?

What if there wasn't?

Caro's expression softened. *You worry too much, sea dog.* "Through here," she said out loud, pointing to the door at the other end of the kitchen. "Take any table you like."

You say that like there's nothing to worry about, Arlo grumbled, and Caro snorted.

You're taking her to dinner. Believe me, the way things work around here, that's better than a good start. It's more than—

Her voice cut off suddenly and she grabbed a passing kitchen hand. "Guts, what the hell're you doing with those desserts? They're—they're melting already!"

Guts looked bewildered as Caro snatched the tray off him and marched off. *What? But those were...* He caught Arlo's eye. *Dumplings. Not desserts...*

Arlo had never seen Caro so off-kilter. *Everything all right?* he sent across the room to her.

She didn't look back. *Enjoy your date with your lady friend, sea dog.*

Arlo's eyebrows drew together as he held the door for Jacqueline. *That didn't sound convincing. I'll ask Tess to talk to her.*

The restaurant wasn't busy, this early in the evening. A few locals were nursing beers or coffees at the shared main table, and a ginger cat was lying stretched out on one of the windowsills. Arlo nodded to him and got a sharp-toothed yawn in reply.

"Is that...?" Jacqueline whispered.

"Tom Hanson. He's been lying there since before I left on the boat, days ago."

Tom's mouth snapped shut. *I'm on bed rest!* he replied, indignant but not so much that he moved any other muscles. *Doctor's orders.*

"He's Marjorie Hanson's grandson, here on break from college," Arlo explained. "Plenty of shifters come here for vacations, just to spend some time in their animal form without worrying about getting caught shifting."

"Oh." Jacqueline's mouth tightened. "I hope no one's worried about me being here. I don't want to make anyone feel as though they're not safe."

"Don't worry," one of the men at the beer-and-coffee table, Carlos, called over. Carlos was the father of the three dolphin shifters Arlo had pointed out to Jacqueline earlier. He was sitting with another local, Dave Oxley.

Arlo relaxed. Carlos was—he hesitated to say "one of the good ones", but he had only moved to Hideaway with his kids a decade or so back. He wasn't one of the old guard like Ma and Pa.

"Harrison already sent around the message," Carlos explained. He raised one hand and counted off his fingers, slightly slowly, as though he was hunting for each number through the bottom of his glass. "One. Lady from Dunston. Two. Came along with those three seal kids. Three..."

"Three, be nice," Dave said, thwacking him gently on the back of the head. "Though that last one was from Harrison's girl." He gave Jacqueline a friendly nod. "They seem like good kids. Be good to have someone who can give your lot a run for their money, eh, Carlos?"

"Pff. Ain't no one can beat my Ana." Carlos Ramirez raised his glass to

111

Jacqueline. "Welcome to Hideaway, miss. And damn, Arlo! Can't wait for the Sweets to hear about this. Tell me you're going to sell tickets to—"

"That's enough of that." Caro swept in from the kitchen, armed with a picnic basket brimming with Tupperware containers. "Here's your order, Carlos. You'd better get it home before your kids start eating the furniture."

Dave gulped the rest of his coffee and bundled the basket under one arm. "I'll look after him, Caro," he said, and cuffed Carlos to his feet. "Come on, man, don't let your kids see you like this."

"It was one beer…" Carlos complained, and blinked. "*Half* of one beer."

"Yeah, and you've got the tolerance of an underweight bee," Dave grumbled good-naturedly, slinging Carlos' arm over his shoulder. "Come on…"

Beside Arlo, Jacqueline stiffened. He put one arm around her. "What's wrong?"

"Oh, it's just… that's something my ex used to say." Jacqueline shook herself. "Not in the same context, though. I'm sure if I'd gotten myself shamefully tipsy on half a glass of beer he'd have…"

She raised her hands. "You know what? I'm going to make a promise to myself right now. No talking about my ex while I'm on the first date in five years." Her hands dropped. "Or make that ten, because—no, I'm not doing this. I'm enjoying the moment." She took a deep breath. "Maybe I'm still not ready. Or I've left it too long. I should have done some practice… windows… before now."

Despite the anxious edge to her voice, she hadn't pulled away from Arlo's arm. And he didn't want her to.

"I'm glad you didn't," he said, and her hand slipped into his.

"Oh?"

"I'm out of practice, too," he said, his heart hammering. Out of practice? Christ. That was one way of putting it.

Jacqueline smiled. "Good," she said. "Then no teasing if I mess it up."

***

"Oh my God," she moaned some time later. Arlo's toes curled. "Oh. *God*. Mmmm."

Her eyes were closed. Shivers of ecstasy made her eyelashes flutter.

"This is incredible," she breathed. "*So much cheese.*"

She cracked one eye open and hunted out another crispy cheese dumpling from her bowl.

"I'm really sorry," she said as she lifted the dumpling to her mouth. "But after this, I'm wondering if I should—*mmm*—be asking Caro on a date instead."

Arlo's wolf whined. He cleared his throat to cover it, even though he knew there was no way Jacqueline would be able to hear it.

"Good luck," he said. "Caro's married to this place."

"Damn." Jacqueline sipped broth from her spoon. "No wonder this is the only restaurant in town. Anywhere else would go out of business in a second."

"You know, I worked here for a bit when I first arrived in Hideaway. The couple who took me in wanted to make sure I had a skill to build a career on."

"They sound like good people."

"They… are. They've done a lot for Hideaway. They're my pack," Arlo said, his voice becoming more confident.

"Your pack? Is that another—" Jacqueline cut herself off. "God, I must sound like the nosiest person in the world."

"What's wrong with that?"

"You live in a secret shifter town! Shouldn't you keep your secrets… secret?"

"Bit late for that."

Jacqueline bit her lips over a smile. "I guess."

Arlo put down his spoon and set his elbows on the table. "You saved Tally's life without thinking. You helped those kids get to a place they'll be safe for the rest of their lives. You've every right to ask questions about what their lives will be like." *Because you're my mate. Everything you want, I'll give you.*

Jacqueline bit her lower lip. "All right." She was silent for a moment, and then: "So. Pack. That's a shifter thing? Like a wolf pack?"

"For me, yeah. Since I'm a wolf." Arlo grinned, so fast and sharp he surprised himself, and then he realized it was his wolf grinning through him. *Thrilled to be part of the conversation, buddy?*

Aroo!

"A very handsome wolf," Jacqueline said, straight-faced, and Arlo's wolf spun around in delight as the back of his neck burned red-hot.

"Pack is family. The people you'd do anything for. Some shifters, those of us whose animals are meant to live in groups, aren't happy without pack around. Whether that's someone to look after, or be looked after by. Or a mate, which is both."

If his skin wasn't already burning, it would have caught fire at that. Jacqueline's eyebrows drew together.

Arlo's jaw tightened. *Oh God. I shouldn't have said anything. Now she'll—*

Arlo's senses went on high alert. The restaurant was busier now than it had been earlier in the evening. Most of the tables were full. Guts and Caro were constantly back and forth from the kitchen, and she'd even managed to prod Tom into taking people's orders.

It was busy, but noisy. Even shifters would find it hard to pick out a conversation from a neighboring table. And other shifters weren't as sensitive to emotions as he was, thank Christ.

He could tell her. A bit. And later, when they were somewhere a bit more private...

The restaurant door opened, letting in a burst of cool air from outside. Arlo shook himself. Why was this bothering him so much? He should want to tell her. *Need* to tell her. why was he so afraid?

Jacqueline leaned forward. "So... A mate?"

"Arlo?"

Too late, Arlo realized who had walked in the door.

CHAPTER FIFTEEN
Jacqueline

*J*acqueline hadn't seen the woman come in, but it was impossible to miss her now that she was standing right behind Arlo. She was short and curvy, with dark hair tied back in a braided bun and thick-rimmed glasses.

She was staring at Arlo with an expression of grim determination.

"Tess?" Arlo said, turning in his seat. He muttered something under his breath and turned an apologetic look on Jacqueline. "I'm sorry about this. I said I'd talk to her later, but…"

Jacqueline recognized the woman now, although her hair wasn't hidden under a hairnet anymore. "She's your not-niece, right?"

"Foster sister, yeah." Arlo sighed and waved Tess over.

"Hi," Tess said, her determination fluttering slightly at the edges. "You're… Jacqueline?"

"That's me." Jacqueline shook Tess's hand.

"I'm sorry for running off earlier. I thought… I don't know." She wiped her hands on her pants and Jacqueline felt a pang of sympathy. Tess was clearly stressing about something—even if Jacqueline didn't know what.

"Tess, we're a bit busy," Arlo said in an undertone.

"I know, I know you said later, but I've been sitting in the shop worrying all afternoon!" She wrung her hands together. "How long have you known? Did you only bring her now because you knew Grandma and Grandpa would be away? Oh, God, Arlo, why didn't you *say* something?"

"Tess-I-met-her-*yesterday*," Arlo gritted out bullet-fast.

"Oh!" Tess said. And then: "Oh-h-h."

Her eyes skidded slowly across to meet Arlo's. Jacqueline could only guess what they said to each other, in that weird silent telepathy, or mindspeak or whatever it was, but Tess covered her mouth and groaned.

"I am so sorry. I am going to go home, and hide in the pantry, and never speak to anyone ever again," she whispered through her fingers. "Except..." Her eyes narrowed. "Maybe this isn't terrible after all. Maybe this is the kick in the pants I need to put my plan into action."

"Your plan...?" Arlo buried his head in his hands. "I don't want to know, do I." It wasn't a question.

"It was nice to meet you!" Tess said to Jacqueline. She grimaced at Arlo, waved, and hurried away, her horrified panic replaced by determination.

"She seems nice," Jacqueline said as the door slammed behind her. "But what did she mean about you waiting until your parents were away?"

Arlo looked abashed. "Tess thinks I've been hiding you away."

"Seriously? I know I joked about feeling like a teenager again, but..."

"My folks are..." Arlo lifted his head. She couldn't read the expression in his eyes. Half-amused, half-pained, half...

Her heart fluttered.

"Jacqueline, there's something I need to tell you." He paused and winced. "Several somethings. Can we walk outside?"

***

It was a cool, still night. The wind that had whipped her hair into a knotted frizz earlier had died down.

Jacqueline and Arlo walked arm-in-arm down the promenade.

Whatever Arlo had meant to say, he wasn't saying it.

"So," Jacqueline said, to break the silence. "Your folks?"

"They'd be… surprised I was with a non-shifter." Arlo's voice was gruff. "But they'll get over it."

He sounded strangely serious. "I guess opportunities to date humans are pretty thin on the ground here in Hideaway," Jacqueline said, lightly.

"I've never dated. A lot of shifters don't, unless…"

Jacqueline's heart thudded. *Unless what? This is just a fling, right? Just a crazy, weekend, casual…*

…Meet his friends, see his workplace, personal tour of his hometown…

Fling?

She swallowed. If this was something that *wasn't* a fling, then there were things she'd have to tell him. Awful things. Like the fact she couldn't have children.

The lump in her throat grew.

She already felt so comfortable around Arlo. Like they fit together. Even his weird date, taking her climbing around the hills behind the town, had unlocked a part of her she'd almost forgotten about, stuck in suburban Dunston. Standing there looking over the town and the sea, panting for breath with the wind in her hair, she'd felt… free.

Because I am free. No more mortgage, no more Derek. I'm free to do whatever I want and what I want is—

"Jacqueline? Is everything all right?"

Arlo's voice was concerned. Jacqueline pulled herself together.

"I…" She searched his eyes. *Is everything all right? It is, isn't it?* "This weekend's been so strange, and I…"

Cocktails. Stupid dresses and high heels. The chance to be sexy again, to find out who I am now. That was the plan. That's what this weekend was about, wasn't it?

She took a deep breath.

I know what I want.

She slid one hand up Arlo's chest, slowly, and the thud of his heartbeat against her palm seemed to echo in her ears. She leaned closer to him and stood on her toes. Arlo's eyes were like deep pools reflecting the night sky. His lips were an inch from hers—less—

Arlo pulled her close and kissed her. His lips were soft, gentle against hers and then harder as she clenched her fist in his shirt. She wound her other hand up over his shoulder, holding herself up against him. Not wanting to ever let him go.

She made a small noise of disappointment as Arlo's lips left hers, and his eyes went dark with lust.

Oh God.

Desire surged through her, so intense her knees went weak. And from the expression in Arlo's eyes...

She got the feeling that whatever he'd been about to say, it could wait.

Jacqueline licked her lips. "You know," she said, her voice hoarse, "I never booked that bed-and-breakfast. I don't have anywhere to stay tonight."

Arlo's fingers tightened around her waist. "That's where you're wrong," he growled.

Jacqueline felt so giddy as they walked back to the *Hometide*, she was half-worried she'd walk straight off the wharf into the sea. She wasn't entirely convinced that if she looked down, she'd see her feet touching the ground.

Arlo handed her onto the boat and slipped the tie rope off its mooring. The *Hometide* eased through the waves. Arlo sat by the rudder and Jacqueline curled into his side, winding her fingers through his.

When Hideaway Cove was a half-moon of lights lying on the horizon, he dropped the anchor and turned to her.

"Jacqueline," he murmured. "I want—ever since I first saw you..."

He pulled her close, kissing her with a growl that made her insides quiver. Jacqueline kissed her back, gasping as he slid one hand up towards her breast... and stopped.

"Hmm?" Jacqueline mumbled against his lips. "What's wrong?"

"Nothing's wrong." Arlo sounded out of breath. "I just..."

His hand smoothed down her side, slow and sensual.

"I don't want to rush," he said. "I want to know what feels good to you. I want to learn everything about your body, every..." He took a tense breath.

Jacqueline ran her fingers through his hair as his eyes dropped. "What is it?"

"I want to do this right. For you. I haven't..." A brief half-smile flickered across his features. "I haven't made a stained glass window before," he admitted.

Does he mean what I think he means?

"What? But..." *That's ridiculous,* Jacqueline stopped herself from saying, to this strong, careful man who'd let himself be so vulnerable in front of her. "I assumed... I mean, you built a *boat*... wait, this metaphor is getting out of control." She sucked in her breath.

"I did build a boat," Arlo agreed. "I built a whole life here. It didn't leave much time for... other arts and crafts."

His voice was still rough, almost ashamed, but the corner of his mouth curved in a tentative, hopeful smile. Jacqueline touched the dimple that formed in his cheek.

"I want to learn about your body," she whispered, trailing her fingertips down his cheek and over his jaw. "I don't care what you've done, or haven't done. It's been so long I feel like I've forgotten it all anyway."

She kissed him until his breathing hitched and then murmured against his lips: "I want to explore it all with you for the first time."

Arlo groaned. "God, yes."

He stood up, lifting her in his arms. Jacqueline wrapped her legs around his waist and heat raced through her. "Downstairs?" she gasped. He nodded.

It was a tight fit, but Arlo maneuvered them both down the ladder without so much as brushing her head against the ceiling. He put her down so gently Jacqueline still felt as though she was floating feet above the floor.

This wasn't her first time. She'd only ever been with Derek, but it wasn't as though they'd had a dead bedroom. They'd had clumsy figuring-it-out sex when they first got together, exhausted wedding-day sex and increasingly good honeymoon sex, lazy sleep-in sex and crazy late-night sex and…

…Rigorously scheduled sex, increasingly clinical sex, sex where she'd found herself thinking a turkey baster would be more efficient or at least more pleasant…

But that was then. And this was now, and now she was with Arlo, and sex could be something thrilling and wonderful again, and her skin was singing with the need to be touched.

And to touch.

Arlo was watching her, still tentative. She stepped forward and slid her hands under his shirt. His abs were smooth and hard under her fingertips, his skin so hot she gasped.

He shivered under her touch. "Too slow?" she asked.

"Don't stop."

Jacqueline looked up at him through her lashes. She smiled and kept exploring.

Arlo had a dark treasure trail that disappeared behind his belt. She ignored it—for now—and moved her hands further up. When she got to his chest, she couldn't hold back from pressing her whole palms against his pecs and sighing.

"God, Jacqueline," Arlo gasped. She pushed his shirt up further, pulling it off over his head and ran her hands over his shoulders, down his back, everywhere she could reach.

"You're incredible," she murmured, kissing his collarbone and dipping her head to lay more kisses down his chest. "I can't stop touching you."

He was so hot under her hands, firm and strong and unbelievably, inconceivably *real*. This was what she'd wanted for so long. What she'd been scrimping and saving for. Taking life by the horns.

Or, in this case…

The sight of Arlo's treasure trail had sparked an idea in her head. She let her hands drift down until they reached his belt buckle.

"I want to do something for you," she murmured, and got on her knees.

"You…" Arlo gasped and licked his lips. "I've never—you don't have to if you don't want…"

"I want to. So much. Do you?" If he'd never been with anyone before…

Jacqueline's skin warmed. She'd never thought *she* would be the one with more knowledge about, well, anything.

"Yes." Arlo's voice was hoarse.

Jacqueline undid his belt buckle slowly, then his flies, and eased his pants down over his hips. Then his boxers. *Like unwrapping a present,* she thought, *and…. Oh, lord…*

Arlo's treasure trail and deep V led down to a cock that made her suddenly ache inside. She wanted him inside her, filling her deep until she couldn't control herself any more. She wanted to touch it, touch *him*. She'd barely touched her wine at the restaurant but she was drunk with joy at finally escaping the paralyzed shell of her life and daring to want something more.

She stroked Arlo's cock, running her fingers along the thick shaft and brushing her lips against its head. He gasped and she turned the brush into a kiss, tasting him, glorying in every shivering breath her mouth and tongue ripped from his body.

She took him in deeper and Arlo moaned so deep she could feel it in her bones. He began to tremble and she pulled back, gazing up at him with her lips just touching his very tip.

He collapsed to his knees in front of her and kissed her, his teeth grazing her hot lips. "Let me do that to you," he begged.

Jacqueline lay back on the bed. There was hardly enough room for Arlo to hold himself above her. He kissed his way down her body, tentative, pausing after he kissed each new part of her to see her reaction. When she gasped out loud as his tongue flicked over her nipple he did it again, harder, until she felt as though he'd barely need to look at her clit for her to come.

He slowed down as he reached her stomach, tantalizingly gentle. He laid a trail of kisses down the crease of her hip and looked up at her.

Jacqueline could hardly breath. The sight of him between her thighs, eyes hot, mouth hotter, almost sent her over the edge.

"Yes," she whispered.

He lowered his head and kissed her.

Sensation flooded out from Jacqueline's clit to fill her whole body and then poured back, intensifying, until each kiss, each lap of his tongue, sent fire through her veins. Pleasure pooled inside her.

"W-wait," she gasped, and Arlo lifted his head. "I want you now. I want to come with you inside me."

He moved up on top of her, his body sliding against hers, his cock bumping against her thigh. His eyes were dark with desire.

"How do you want me to—" he began, and Jacqueline gently pushed him on his side, so they were lying together. She draped one leg over his hip and slowly guided him to her entrance.

"Like this," she whispered.

He pushed into her and she let out a shaking gasp. Arlo was gentle, careful, as though he was worried he might break her, and the expression on his face was unguarded wonder.

She rolled her hips, drawing him deeper and he moaned. Every movement, every sound, made her want him more.

He slid one hand down to her ass and used his grip to anchor her as he thrust in, making her gasp and moan as pleasure swamped her conscious thoughts. He went deeper and deeper, hitting her g-spot with each thrust.

"Oh God," Arlo gasped, and she couldn't stop her body from responding.

Her whole body clenched, ecstasy shuddering through her again and again. Arlo moaned and rolled on top of her. When he thrust again he went even deeper, filling her until she felt like she would explode. Her orgasm was still rolling through her. She cried out as he thrust into her again. Slowly. In control.

Her eyes fluttered open. Arlo gazed down at her, his expression enough to make her wrap her legs more tightly around him and pull him into her again. He groaned, meeting her intensity with her own need, and held her close against himself as he came.

He didn't let her go afterwards, and Jacqueline didn't want him to. She kept her arms around him, feeling the thud of his heartbeat, the ragged pants as he caught his breath. As they both did, their bodies still completely entwined.

"Are you all right?" Arlo asked.

Jacqueline was still panting. She laughed, breathless. "Am I—? Oh, God, Arlo. That was incredible." She pressed her cheek against him. "Am I all right. *Really.*"

He rolled off her, still holding her so they ended up tangled together side by side. "I wanted to be sure. I don't trust myself to pick things up, all the time."

His eyes were dancing. He was teasing her. Jacqueline tsk'ed.

"Well you don't need to worry about that." She snuggled close against him. "That was everything I've been wanting for a long, long time."

He was stroking her back; at her words, he paused. "It's all I've wanted," he murmured.

***

The first thing Jacqueline noticed as she woke up was warmth. Specifically, the solid, reassuring warmth of Arlo's body against her. It was so exactly

124

what she wanted that for a moment she was sure she was in a dream.

She opened her eyes.

Not a dream, she thought, and it was the happiest thought she'd had in a long time.

Arlo was stretched out on his back and she was tucked against him, her head on his shoulder and one arm curled up on his chest. Her fingers twitched before the conscious thought that she wanted to stroke his golden skin even reached her brain, and she forced them to be still. Arlo was still asleep and she wanted to savor this moment as long as possible, before…

Before he wakes up and this perfect moment falls to pieces.

She swallowed a sigh. When she'd imagined her first post-divorce hookup, it sure as hell hadn't been with a ruggedly handsome sailor who could turn into a wolf. She'd envisaged nights on the town, ridiculous cocktails and short glitzy dresses, not a long evening sinking into his eyes over the best meal she'd ever eaten and a slow, sensuous seduction while the sea rocked under them.

Jacqueline shivered as she remembered the way he'd touched her. Tenderly, reverently, as though he was afraid she'd dissolve into mist.

A lump formed in her throat. No, it wasn't what she'd imagined at all. And now…

Arlo's breathing changed. His eyelids fluttered and Jacqueline blinked, driving back the sudden darkness at the edge of her mind.

"Good morning," she whispered.

Arlo's eyes opened. Jacqueline shivered again as he looked at her, the touch of his gaze like slipping into a warm bath.

"You're still here," he murmured, sliding one hand along her waist. Jacqueline laughed.

"What was I going to do, swim away?"

"I mean…" Arlo's eyebrows drew together. "You're here. You're real. The last two days weren't a dream."

Jacqueline's stomach lurched. Two days? Was that all? And she was

125

already—

Arlo pushed himself up on his elbows. "Jacqueline? Are you all right?"

Damn it. Whatever she was feeling, and she wasn't even sure herself what that was, must have shown on her face. She reached for his shoulder and pulled herself to sit up beside him.

How could she explain how quickly she was falling for him, without sounding like a complete psycho?

"It's nothing. Just—"

Arlo suddenly doubled over. He clutched at his head with a strangled shout of pain.

"What's wrong?" Jacqueline wrapped one arm around his shoulder to support him. His muscles were so tense it was like holding onto a knotted tree trunk. "Arlo, what is it?"

"Head," he managed to grunt. "Voices."

"The kids?" Terror knotted in Jacqueline's stomach.

Arlo nodded and winced in pain again.

"We have to get to them." Jacqueline scrambled out of bed and grabbed her clothes from the floor. She pulled them on quickly.

Arlo was following suit, his face taut with pain. He swayed sideways, almost hitting his head on the ladder, and Jacqueline pulled him back to his feet. She wrapped both arms around his waist and held him steady, staring into his eyes.

He let his forehead rest against hers. This close she could tell he was actually trembling.

"Come on," she whispered, her breath shaking. "Let's go get them."

"I can't—" Arlo grimaced, squeezing his eyes tight. "It hurts too much. I can hardly see."

"I'll do the seeing for both of us. You make the boat move, and I'll tell you where to go." Jacqueline put her hands either side of his head. "Trust me. We can do this together."

"I trust you." The words came out on a breath so heavy Jacqueline was only half-sure what he'd said. She pressed her lips against his and felt him shiver.

"Then let's go."

The sun was still low, but Arlo swore under his breath as he climbed up on deck. He made his way to the skipper's seat with one arm up over his eyes. Jacqueline followed on his heels although it was clear he knew where he was going by memory alone.

Arlo collapsed on the seat. "Anchor," he growled, and started to stand up again. Jacqueline put a hand on his chest.

"I'll handle it," she said.

He grasped her hand and held it tight for a moment before letting go. "Thank you," he said, his voice ragged. "It's never been this bad before."

Their eyes met, and a jagged moment of shared realization thundered between them. Jacqueline gulped. *If it's never been this bad before—what's happened?*

Arlo unfurled the sails by feel and they were off the moment the anchor was out of the water. With Jacqueline directing him, Arlo sailed for the tiny beach at the base of the cliff with the lighthouse on top of it.

"I've got Harrison," he groaned, motioning to his temple. "Here. They'll meet us on the beach."

They didn't get that far.

Jacqueline had just dropped anchor. Arlo was hauling on the dinghy's tow rope to bring it close enough to board. An eagle's screech cut through the air and Jacqueline whipped her head up to see something that was definitely not an eagle leap off the top of the cliff.

"Is that a…" she began, grabbing Arlo's arm.

He didn't need to look up. "Harrison," he said. "And Tally. It's her voice."

"Is she hurt?" Jacqueline's throat went tight.

"She's—"

The not-an-eagle unfurled its wings mid-leap. Jacqueline gasped. It was a—she racked her memory for the word. Mandrake? Hippogriff?

Griffin, she thought as it—he—Harrison landed on the deck. The ship rocked under his weight, but Arlo and Jacqueline were already racing towards him.

"Do you have her?"

"What's wrong? What happened?"

"Is she—"

Harrison was holding Tally in his fore claws. She was in her seal shape, wriggling and making a howling, whining noise that made Jacqueline's heart rate rocket.

Jacqueline reached forward and swept her up at the same time Arlo did. They held her sandwiched between them, their arms tangled around her and each other.

"What is it, baby?" Jacqueline asked desperately. "What's wrong?" She looked up at Arlo, whose expression was stricken. "Can you talk to hear? Hear her?"

"She…" Arlo's face relaxed and he leaned forward, resting his forehead against hers. Nestled between them, Tally fell silent. "She's fine. She was lonely, and scared. But she's all right now."

Tally snuffled against Jacqueline's neck. A second later, she turned back into a baby girl, her pale eyes damp with tears.

"Is everything okay now, honey?" Jacqueline ducked her head to look into Tally's face.

"Es," whispered Tally, wrapping her arms around Jacqueline's neck.

Jacqueline caught Arlo's eyes on her and smile. "Is your head feeling better?"

Arlo touched his temple gingerly. "Better. Still tender."

"I'm glad." She looked back down at Tally. "So much fuss just because you were lonely? Weren't your brother and sister here with you?"

Jacqueline looked towards shore. They were close enough that she could make out three figures on the beach: Kenna, Dylan and Lainie.

"Can you tell if they're all right? If Tally's this upset over something—"

128

Arlo cocked his head. "They're mostly worried about her. I'm telling them she's fine."

There was a whoosh of air as Harrison shifted. He marched over to them, frowning.

"What's wrong with your head, Arlo?"

"You didn't feel it?" Arlo looked at Harrison with an expression of surprise that turned into a wince as he swung his head around. "She was so loud, I could hardly hear myself think. And she was so lonely it... hurt. A lot."

"She was loud, sure. But you're the only one with a migraine." Harrison frowned. "Is everything all right, bud?"

Arlo rubbed his forehead. He glanced at Jacqueline, then away, then back at her, as though he couldn't keep his eyes away. "Better than all right," he said, his voice soft.

Warmth flooded through Jacqueline, turning into a smile as Tally chortled against her neck. Jacqueline squeezed her and kissed the top of her head.

"Well, I'm glad it wasn't anything serious. We'd better get back to shore and let the others know." Harrison rolled his shoulders back. "I could fly you over, or—"

"We'll row in," Arlo interrupted, then paused to check with Jacqueline.

She nodded happily. After the scare with Tally, she wasn't sure she could manage something as exciting as flying on a griffin's back—and a short trip in the rowboat might be the last chance she had to salvage a scrap of time with Arlo, before they got back into the bustle of real life.

Tally giggled and Arlo rocked back slightly, blinking.

"She wants to fly," he explained to Jacqueline as Tally shifted back into her seal form and started wriggling. "Harrison, you mind?"

"So long as she doesn't start yelling again," Harrison said gallantly, and tucked Tally under one arm. "Good practice, anyway, right?"

He shifted and leaped into the air in one smooth movement. Jacqueline leaned closer to Arlo.

"I'm assuming that noise she's making is happy?"

"Very." Arlo gazed into her eyes and for a moment, Jacqueline forgot what she'd been about to say. "Jacqueline…"

"Hmm?"

Somehow, their hands found each other's. Jacqueline tangled her fingers around his.

"There's something I want to talk to you about and this might be the only chance we have," he said. "I should have said it earlier, but last night—and now with Tally—I've let every chance slip me by. I won't let that happen again."

Jacqueline raised her eyebrows. "Sounds serious," she said as her heart started beating so hard she was worried Arlo might be able to hear it.

Arlo sighed. "I wanted to tell you this on the *Hometide*. At my workshop. Every minute since I met you. But I…" He shook his head. "I know you've been hurt before."

"I… yes," Jacqueline said slowly. "You could say that."

"You were betrayed by the man who pledged to care for you for the rest of both your lives."

Only because I betrayed him first. Because I couldn't give him the one thing he wanted most from our marriage.

She pushed the treacherous thought away but even with it gone, Jacqueline's chest tightened around her hammering heart. Another joke rose to her lips and she bit it back.

"I don't regret anything that happened last night," she said, instead of the jokey brush-off that had bubbled up at first. Her voice wobbled.

Arlo's eyes sharpened with concern. "That's not—I don't, either," he said, his voice gravelly. His hands tightened around hers. "I could never regret any time spent with you."

Any time? Jacqueline's treacherous mind took the words and spun them out into whole novels. *Any time—meaning more time than just now? More time than just this weekend? Does he want to see me again? Does he want—*

Jacqueline put a lid on her thoughts and pushed it down tight.

Stop over thinking it. Just listen to him.

Arlo took a deep breath. "Last night, you asked me about mates. I didn't answer you."

Jacqueline could see how much effort it was taking him to get the words out, and her heart was so full of sympathy that it took her another moment to realize what he was saying.

"Yes," she said slowly. "I remember."

The lid was coming off her pot of ridiculous thoughts and emotions. She held onto it, just for now, just in case this wasn't going where all those stupid thoughts thought it was going.

"You don't have to say anything now," Arlo said urgently. "I know it's different for humans. Don't feel like you need to answer, or say you feel the same, or—"

"It would help if I knew what it is I'm meant to be having these feelings about," Jacqueline said gently.

"Right." Arlo bowed his head. When he looked up, his expression was more vulnerable than Jacqueline had ever seen before. "Every shifter has a soulmate. One person, somewhere in the world, who's the other half of their heart. Shifters know who their mate is from the moment they first set eyes on them. And I knew from the moment I first set eyes on you. Every second since then has made me more sure. You're my mate."

Jacqueline swallowed. Suddenly, her eyes were swimming, and the only words she could find were a choked: "You're sure?"

"I am. God, Jacqueline, I am. But you don't have to be. I know it's too sudden, you have your own things going on." She saw Arlo grimace through the shimmer of tears. "I should have told you earlier. This is the wrong time, the wrong place, I—"

"Will you shut up for one second!" Jacqueline pulled her hands away from his and threw them around his shoulders. He was warm and solid and she buried her face in his chest, her lungs heaving. "These are happy tears."

"Oh." Arlo dropped his head to rest on hers and wrapped his arms around her.

Jacqueline smiled. "Is that a good oh?"

Arlo let out a sigh that seemed to shake his bones. "God, yes."

"Good." Jacqueline sniffled. "And don't worry. I always cry when I'm too happy and this is... so much, all at once."

"Too much?" Arlo stiffened. "I meant what I said. Anything you need, time, space, even if—" He took a sharp breath. "If you don't feel the same way..."

If I don't feel like what? Like I knew I'd met my soulmate the moment he pulled me out of the sea?

Jacqueline took a slow breath, her face still buried in Arlo's shirt. He smelled like salt and sweat, and she never wanted to breathe in anything else ever again.

"When I first saw you," she said, "don't laugh—I didn't see you at all. I was out of my mind with fear. I thought I'd gone. I'd just seen kids turn into animals and I jumped in the water, almost got myself killed, trying to save something I was sure shouldn't even exist."

"Why would I laugh at that?"

"Because as soon as you grabbed me, I wasn't scared anymore." She hadn't even thought about it at the time. But it was true. As soon as she'd felt Arlo's touch, some deep part of her had known she was safe. "I wasn't scared of drowning. I wasn't scared I'd gone mad and started seeing things. I wasn't even scared to harangue you until you let me go with you!"

"I didn't need much haranguing," Arlo pointed out.

"I didn't think there could be any reason you'd let me come with you. And I desperately wanted to. I wanted it more than anything I've ever wanted in my life." She swallowed. "*That* scared me. Wanting something that much."

132

Wanting something, and knowing that wanting something with that much of my being is a surefire way to make sure the universe never gives it to me.

"And now?"

Jacqueline stood on her tiptoes until she could kiss him. "Now I know why I want to stick around so badly."

We're meant to be together. Soulmates.

He's been here all this time. Waiting for me.

She blinked. Her eyelashes were still wet, and she tried to draw back enough to wipe her eyes, but Arlo held her close.

"If you're staying, then I'm not letting go of you just yet."

Jacqueline dropped down off her tiptoes and laughed into his shirt. "Fine. Have it your way."

She let herself melt against him, every curve of her body contouring to his muscular form. Arlo groaned deep in his throat.

"What happens next?" Jacqueline asked. "I mean, I can feel what *you* want to happen next..."

Arlo swore under his breath and maneuvered his lower half away from her. Jacqueline laughed and pressed herself up close to him again.

"I don't know," Arlo said, sounding honestly baffled. "I didn't think this would go so easy."

"With a human?"

"With anyone." Arlo's voice was rueful. "My life's been one wrong turn after another. Hideaway Cove was the first good decision I made, and part of me thought that was it, I'd used up my quota. But you... you're more than I ever dreamed of."

"Maybe we're both having a fresh start," Jacqueline suggested.

"I like that. As for what happens next, I'd suggest we sail off into the sunset," Arlo said, one hand stroking up Jacqueline's back to cup the back of her head, "but it's the wrong time of day for that."

Jacqueline bit her lip. A whole day of sailing with Arlo, watching the sun travel across the sky, the slow build of sensuous anticipation as they found a place to weigh anchor for the night and go to bed…

Arlo groaned. "We have an audience," he whispered in Jacqueline's ear.

"Oh." Jacqueline twisted to look past him, to the beach. "So much for sailing off into the sunset. Tally'd probably kick up another fuss if we were gone that long, anyway, and I don't want you struck down by another migraine just when you got over that one."

Jacqueline brushed the backs of her fingers over Arlo's temple. She'd meant it light-heartedly, but he frowned.

"I don't know what it is. Harrison isn't as badly affected."

"Maybe he just needs a longer exposure. You said you had her banging on your skull all day Friday."

"True…" His eyes caught hers, warm and tender. "You care about them."

"Of course I do! How could I not? I don't think I'll feel like I've done my job here until they're settled. And I'm glad the Sweets are going to look after them until we track Eric down." She slipped her arms around his waist. "You say they half-raised you and given how you turned out, they must know what they're doing."

"Right." Arlo's jaw tightened. "Yes."

He pulled her close again, his arms strong around her. Jacqueline sighed happily. Even just being held by Arlo made her feel safe. Grounded, somehow, even though they were on the water.

For the first time in a long time and despite all the magic, and dragons who messed with electricity, and seal shifters who gave people psychic headaches, Jacqueline felt as though she'd finally found a piece of the world where she fit perfectly into place.

CHAPTER SIXTEEN
Arlo

Jacqueline was so obviously happy as Arlo rowed them both to the beach that he couldn't tell her what was weighing on his mind.

The Sweets.

Dorothy and Alan Sweets had taken care of him when he washed up in Hideaway a hopeless, helpless teenager, that was true. But their ironclad protectiveness for shifters was matched by an equal lack of trust for humans. He had to warn Jacqueline that things might get tense when she met them and he told them who she was.

Later, he promised. *When we're not around everyone. When she's had a chance to get to grips with… everything else.*

The Sweets were away for the weekend. He had time.

He helped Jacqueline out of the rowboat and shot Harrison an accusing glare over his shoulder. The kids' excited anticipation was so intense he could almost see it.

"Don't just stand there like you don't know what's up," he growled.

Lainie laughed and clapped her hands together. "No, you don't get off that easily! We want to hear you say it."

"You all already know?" Jacqueline leaned against Arlo as she got her footing on the soft sand.

Dylan was jumping on the spot. Tally was standing next to him, in human form, and every time he jumped she bobbed up and down in imitation. Even Kenna was failing to hide an ear-to-ear grin.

"How is anyone meant to keep any secrets around here?" Jacqueline asked, laughing.

Arlo's chest constricted. Luckily, Harrison answered for him.

"If you want to keep something like this a secret, you need to be a bit subtler about it than Arlo here. Even the kids picked it up. Right, Kenna?"

A prickle of uncertainty zipped off Kenna, but she caught it so quickly Arlo wasn't sure if he'd imagined it.

"Yeah," she said out loud, shrugging. "It was pretty obvious. He looked like he'd been smacked in the face with a fish."

"If that's not romantic, then what is," deadpanned Lainie. She nodded at Arlo. "Come on. No getting off the hook."

Arlo took a deep breath that felt like it aired out his entire soul.

"Lainie, Harrison—kids…" he began, and found himself grinning so wide he could barely get the words out. "This is my mate. Jacqueline March."

"And this," Jacqueline echoed him, wrapping one arm around his waist. "is mine. Arlo Hammond."

Her eyes sparkled brighter than the sun on the waves.

"Jacqueline March, from that little town across the hill? How lovely. I believe I know your colleague, Deirdre," announced a thin, educated voice from the shadows in the tunnel that led up to the top of Lighthouse Hill.

Arlo's shoulders tensed. He knew that voice better than the back of his hand.

"Well, Arlo? Do introduce us. I might have heard of Jacqueline but I don't believe we've actually met."

136

Ma Sweets stepped out of the shadows. She was wearing her driving outfit, a neat aubergine skirt suit with a lilac scarf over her perfectly coifed hair. Her husband, Alan, wandered out behind her, looking as usual one good yawn away from falling asleep on his feet.

Arlo cleared his throat. "Jacqueline," he said, trying not to show how much he was panicking, "these are my foster parents, Dorothy and Alan Sweets."

She's human, he added, speaking directly to the two alligator shifters, *and she's my mate. I won't have you say anything against her.*

Dear, why would I say anything like that? Ma Sweets replied, and the skin on the back of Arlo's neck prickled.

***

Lainie set the table. Rather, it looked as though she'd been halfway through setting the breakfast table when Tally woke up and started crying. She put out an extra two places, reluctance in every line of her body.

"So you know Deirdre?" Jacqueline said, sounding cheerful.

"Through bridge." Ma Sweets inclined her head. "Which is why we were absent this weekend. It is *such* a good way to keep abreast of what's happening in the neighborhood. But of course we left the tournament as soon as Sharon called us with the news."

Sharon Warbol was a plover shifter, and one of Ma Sweets' oldest friends.

"Why the rush?" Arlo asked.

Ma Sweets opened her eyes wide. "To meet the children, of course! And it will do Deirdre good to win a tournament for once, poor dear." She smiled at the kids and they shuffled their feet.

"Food's up," Lainie announced, sweeping between Ma Sweet and the kids. "Hope you all like pancakes."

The atmosphere lightened as they all dug into the food. Ma Sweets managed to maneuver herself into sitting next to Jacqueline, but refrained from saying anything rude about humans, even when Kenna retold the story about how they'd had to run away from their human foster home.

"Well." Ma Sweets winked at Kenna conspiratorially. "What a time you've all had! But never to worry. Pa and I are here now, and we'll make sure you never have to do anything like that again."

Kenna frowned. "But—"

"Sharon didn't tell you?" Arlo cut in smoothly. His wolf's coat was prickling with that sense of wrongness again. "They didn't do it all on their own. They don't need a foster home, just somewhere to rest up until their uncle Eric gets here."

Dylan wriggled in his seat and Arlo knew what was coming. He shot a warning at Kenna before she told Dylan to shut up and her mouth snapped shut in a surprised scowl.

"What's up, Dylan?"

"He's not *really* our uncle…"

Arlo rubbed his forehead. Jacqueline leaned forward. "Who is he, then?"

"He's just… another shifter… who found us, and said he'd look after us, and take us somewhere safe…"

Until he abandoned you. Arlo gritted his teeth.

"But he *is* responsible for you, isn't he, my dear? He's your pack leader," said Ma Sweets, nodding.

"Y-yes?" Dylan's answer sounded more like a question. This time, Arlo wasn't fast enough to stop Kenna from kicking him under the table. "I mean…"

"What do you mean, pack leader?" Jacqueline said, frowning. "If he's not related to you, I'm afraid I'm going to have some trouble explaining to my boss how you all ran away and ended up here."

Her eyes met Arlo's and he could imagine what she was stopping herself from saying: that it would be even more difficult to convince the county to let the kids stay.

"But that's no problem at all, my dear!" Ma Sweets trilled.

138

"But he'll need to be registered as a foster parent. And—" Jacqueline's expression tightened. "That's *hard*, there are a lot of hoops to jump through…"

"Oh, *paperwork.*" Dorothy Sweets waved the idea away with a dismissive gesture. "Required to keep the county off our backs, yes, but we all know it's not *really* important." She tapped the back of Jacqueline's hand with one pointed fingertip. "*Pack.* That's all that really matters. The bonds that all shifters innately understand. Any shifter would move heaven and earth for their pack. And rest assured, we will make *absolutely certain* that this little pack receives all the help they need to settle here in Hideaway Cove."

She tapped Jacqueline's hand again. "Pack is the *one thing*, my dear, that we shifters value above all else. Don't you all agree?"

At the other end of the table, Harrison cleared his throat. "I don't know about that," he said, spearing a steak and exchanging a look with Lainie. "All sounds a bit wolfy to me. What do you think, Lainie? Are we pack?"

"Nest, maybe," Lainie suggested, wrinkling her nose. "Or—i-ree? Ee-rie? However you say that word. Eyrie." She turned to Dorothy and wrinkled her brow. "Would you say alligators have 'packs', Mrs. Sweets? Or is there a better term we should use for you?"

"The word isn't important," Dorothy snapped. "What is important is that, as shifters, we all look out for one another."

"That's right," Arlo interjected. He was starting to feel like the conversation was getting away from him. "And that includes our mates."

He took Jacqueline's hand and she smiled at him.

"Does that make me pack, then?" she asked.

Yes, Arlo's wolf yipped. *Pack!*

"Of course," Ma Sweets cooed. "We're all so looking forward to Arlo and you starting a little pack of your own. I know it's what he's wanted ever since he came here."

"That's true," Arlo admitted. He felt as though the sun was rising in his head. Of course. Of *course* that was what had been grating away at the inside of his skull.

Jacqueline dropped her fork.

The hairs on the back of Arlo's neck prickled. Ma Sweets was smiling, but Jacqueline had gone pale. Arlo bent to pick up Jacqueline's fork and brought his head close to hers.

"Are you all right?" he asked.

"Fine." Jacqueline's smile was tight. Arlo straightened, feeling uneasy.

"And when is it you're due?" Ma Sweets asked Lainie.

"A few months away still," Lainie replied, one hand on her bump.

"How lovely. It will be nice to have another griffin shifter around the place. Or a little human, of course." Dorothy shrugged delicately.

"Those aren't the only options," Lainie replied, her fingers white-knuckled on her cutlery.

"Excuse me," Jacqueline blurted out, and stood up so quickly she caught herself on the tablecloth. Arlo rose to help her, but she was already halfway out the door.

"Oh dear," said Dorothy. "I hope she didn't eat something that disagreed with her."

Arlo glanced at her over his shoulder as he headed for the door, and his wolf *snarled*. Ma Sweets' eyebrows shot up, and Pa actually woke up.

What the hell was that? Arlo asked his wolf as he raced after Jacqueline. It was still growling low in its throat, as though it expected Ma Sweets to jump out and ambush them.

More importantly, what's wrong with Jacqueline?

He found her in the bathroom, standing propped over the sink. Her eyes flew to his in the mirror.

"What's wrong?" Arlo asked, and she looked away. He touched her arm and she pulled away, folding her arms in front of herself.

"I should have known it was too good to be true," she whispered. She heaved a breath and straightened, turning to face him but still not looking him in the eye.

140

"Please tell me what's wrong. I'll do whatever you need to help." Arlo's heart was breaking. Just a few minutes before, Jacqueline had been laughing with Lainie, and now she looked as though her world was falling apart. "Anything. Just talk to me, please."

"All right." Even Jacqueline's voice was guarded. She squeezed her eyes shut and opened them again, almost but not quite meeting his eyes, as though she was trying to but couldn't quite force herself to. Her gaze settled somewhere over his shoulder. "Is what Dorothy said true? You want a family. A *whole* family. Kids."

Pack, Arlo's wolf barked, and before Arlo could stop himself or connect the dots, he said, "Of course. Wolves are pack animals. I *need* a pack."

And I'd do a better job than this Eric bastard.

"Oh. Well. Good," Jacqueline blurted, the words falling like bricks. "Good, that's, that's—that's good to know." She broke off suddenly and pressed her hands against her eyes. "*Shit.*"

"Jacqueline, for God's sake, tell me what's going on," Arlo pleaded. His instincts were screaming at him to help her, but he didn't know how. He reached out for her again and she flinched back.

Arlo stepped back and she raised her hands, palms out.

"I'm sorry," she said, her voice scratchy, "I'm sorry, I need to go."

"If you need time, you just need to say," Arlo reminded her. "I know this is a lot to take in—"

Jacqueline made a noise that was half laugh, half sob. "Time isn't going to help. This isn't anything new to take in. It's the same old—it doesn't matter." Her hands dropped. "It doesn't matter."

"Yes, it does." Hesitantly, Jacqueline's unhappiness like a scar twisting in his chest, Arlo stepped forward and put his arms around her. This time, she let him. Her head fell to rest against his chest.

Arlo held her gently. For a few seconds she didn't say anything, just breathed. He could feel her heart hammering through her back. Somewhere in the house, a phone rang.

Then she shook her head and pushed herself away from him. Her eyes were dry, and hard, like windows with the shutters closed over them.

"Arlo, I…"

Someone knocked on the door. "Jacqueline? Sorry to interrupt." It was Lainie, holding a cordless phone. "It's for you."

Arlo was about to say *Now isn't a good time* when Lainie caught his eye. Even he could see the steel in her gaze.

He'd told her he wouldn't hurt Jacqueline. And he had. Somehow. He'd failed at the most important thing a shifter needed to do: protecting his mate.

Shame twisted in his gut as Jacqueline ducked around him and took the phone.

"Hello? Oh, Reg… yes… Of course I've heard, I called you about them, remember? Oh…"

She listened to the phone for a few more minutes and then hung up. She took a deep breath that pulled at Arlo's heart—

—and turned to Lainie.

"That was the sheriff," she said, not even glancing at Arlo. "He's found Eric and has him at the station. Could we go and pick him up now, do you think? I know it's no notice at all but—"

"The kids need him." Lainie nodded.

"And…" Jacqueline's eyes did flick to Arlo now, but the pain in them made it hurt more than her ignoring him had. "I should go too. I think it would be best if I was there to vouch for him with the sheriff."

She held her arms straight at her sides, fists clenched.

Arlo's mouth was dry. "I can drive you—"

"No." Her voice was final. "Please. Let me go. You have to—this is for the best. I promise." Her shoulders slumped. "If you want to know more, ask your mom. I can't talk about it. Not now."

Everything moved too quickly after that. It was like looking underwater, with the light bending his perception of everything. Arlo felt constantly half a second behind everyone else.

Then the Land Rover's engine roared, and the world snapped back into focus.

CHAPTER SEVENTEEN
Jacqueline

"You might want to blink at some point."

She'd been listening to nothing but the sound of the Land Rover's tires on the road that it took Jacqueline a moment to notice Harrison was talking to her.

"Blink?"

Harrison was staring straight ahead at the road. "You've been staring into space ever since we got in the car, and that was a few hours ago. Your eyeballs must be dry as a bone."

At least I'm not crying. Jacqueline gnawed on the inside of her cheek. She didn't cry, though, not when she was sad. She got like this: eyes hot and dry, face and neck aching with tension. If she fell asleep without forcing herself to relax, she'd wake up with a three-day headache.

It was all so... familiar.

She made herself blink. Her eyes stung, but she still didn't cry.

I'm still the same person I was before. I was stupid to think that any new life I had, any new relationship, would be any different to before.

Jacqueline sighed and pressed her hands against her eyes. "Sorry. I haven't exactly been a thrilling conversationalist during this drive."

"Do you want to talk about it?"

"No." *Talking won't help.* She dropped her hands in her lap. "Oh—you'll want to turn here. If you go in on the main road, you'll get caught up going through all the rest of town before we make it to the sheriff's office."

"You know, sometimes I'm happy to live in a town with a single two-lane street, and some days I'm downright ecstatic." Harrison turned into the street Jacqueline had indicated. "It took Lainie a few weeks to really get her head around the idea that there's no 'next block over' in Hideaway. Things are either a ways down the street, or a few hours' drive to the next town."

Jacqueline closed her eyes briefly. *I can see where this is going.* "Next right," she said out loud.

"Thanks." Harrison was quiet for a moment. "You know, some things take time to…"

"Please don't. Whatever you're about to say."

Harrison sighed. "The Sweets are… well. Difficult. But not everyone in Hideaway Cove thinks the way they do. Whatever happens, Lainie and I will have your back. And Arlo will, that goes without saying."

Jacqueline didn't know what to say. Lainie and Harrison didn't know a thing about her, but they were on her side? There was no one in Dunston she could expect that of.

Because they still think you and Arlo will end up together. Jacqueline couldn't speak past the lump in her throat. Harrison thought Arlo would have her back?

She had his. That's why she was doing this. Better to cut it off now than leave things to fester.

"Th-thanks," she managed. "Sheriff's just up ahead."

Harrison pulled up outside and Jacqueline almost jumped out of the car, she was so glad to exit the conversation. Movement flickered behind one of the front windows and Jacqueline waved.

Home again.

Her whole body felt heavy, but it was easy to plaster on a smile. After all, this was no worse than coming back to work after Derek left, was it? At least no one here knew that she'd failed to make the grade for another man.

The office was quiet; just Deirdre at the desk, with the green reflection in her glasses giving away the fact that she was playing bridge on her computer, not doing work, and the sound of Reg somewhere in the back. Jacqueline interrupted Deirdre long enough to introduce her to Harrison and was about to ask after Eric when Reg burst through the door.

"There she is! You're here for the runaway?" Reg didn't wait for her to answer. He swept past her and pumped Harrison's hand. "And here's the man to complain to, I'm guessing. Harrison Galway? Pleased to meet you. Reg Hunt. So, you're mayor down there these days, eh? How you finding that in, ah…"

Talking to Reg was like having a train bearing down on you. A train that occasionally needed a nudge back onto the tracks.

"Hideaway Cove," Jacqueline muttered.

"Cove! Just the word I was after." Reg snapped his fingers. "And what brings you—ah, yes, of course. Sending the big man to give the truant a hard word, eh?"

He punched Harrison on the arm and then gestured for them both to follow him. Jacqueline almost lost her professional face as he pushed through the door to the cells.

"Boss, don't tell me you've been holding him back here all weekend?"

"Well, you asked us to keep an eye out for him," Reg replied, winking.

"Not to lock him up!"

"Is that really necessary?" Harrison asked Reg.

"Nowhere else for him," Reg announced cheerfully. "It'll do him good, anyway. Scare him back on the straight and narrow."

146

Anger pulsed in Jacqueline's temples. "Really."

And now I get to explain to the poor guy why calling me for help got him put in the lockup for the weekend. If I'd only come back sooner, not spent the extra night in Hideaway. I could have gotten this one thing sorted out without hurting anyone.

Except then I'd still think I had a chance with Arlo. At least this way, I've gotten that over with.

Reg was still talking. "You know kids—well, no, maybe you don't. If you had your own, you'd understand. Tough love, that's what they need."

Hang on—kids?

"Here we go. The Lost Boy himself. Say hi, kid."

Jacqueline's heart sank as she saw the figure sitting in the cell. "Eric?"

The man raised his head and Jacqueline's heart sank even further. Eric wasn't a grown man, no matter what the Weaver kids had said.

She rounded on Reg. "You've had him here all weekend? He can't be more than sixteen!"

Reg's eyebrows almost shot off his head.

That must be the closest I've gotten to raising my voice at him all the years I've worked here, Jacqueline thought. *Well, he deserves it!*

"Nineteen, it says on his license," he replied. "Which is somewhere about."

And how real is that license? Jacqueline wondered. From the expression on Harrison's face, he was thinking the same thing.

Harrison cleared his throat and walked over to the cell.

"Hey, Eric. My name's Harrison. I think you and Ms. March here have already spoken."

Eric looked confused. "On the phone," Jacqueline prompted, and relief and anxiety flooded across his face in equal measure. He stood up and hurried to the bars.

"Did you—" he began, and then anxiety won the battle. He fell silent, eyes huge.

"They're all waiting for you in Hideaway Cove," Jacqueline reassured him. "Tally, Dylan and Kenna."

"Oh, thank you. Thank you so much." Eric's head dropped against the bars. "I've been so worried. I only meant to be gone a few nights. I only meant to go for groceries but my car broke down after the storm, and I got a lift to just out of town but I—" His eyes slid sideways past Jacqueline, to where Reg was leaning against a desk. "I guess I didn't explain my problem very well," he muttered.

God, the poor guy. He's the one who's been holding the kids together for the last few months? I thought he sounded young on the phone, but I thought that was just the panic making his voice squeaky.

He wasn't another Weaver sibling, that was for sure, with his dark skin and eyes. His hair was cut close to his scalp, which was probably meant to be part of his looking-older-than-he-was act. He had huge, puppy-dog eyes that he kept squinted half-shut as he looked between Harrison and Jacqueline, probably for the same reason.

Eric was tall and loose-limbed, with the sort of lanky build that must have his parents worried how much more growing he had to do. Except he was here, locked up in Reg's drunk tank, and he'd spent the last how-many weeks on the run with three shifter kids.

Parents probably not in the picture, Jacqueline determined, wrapping her arms around herself. *There is far too much of that going around.*

"Let's get you out of here and back to Hideaway Cove," Harrison said garrulously.

"But I'm not from—"

"Back *home,*" Harrison said, with emphasis, and Jacqueline got the feeling he backed it up with some mindspeak reassurances. Eric's eyes unsquinted again and he nodded vigorously.

"Now, Sheriff…" Harrison began, and within ten minutes had somehow managed to smooth everything over. Somehow even Reg not being able to find a pen or remember his computer password to log Eric in the system turned into him maybe letting the whole thing slide this time after all.

Jacqueline would have been seething—he'd had Eric in lockup overnight and hadn't even *booked* it?—but this was a good result. Eric was going back to Hideaway. All the kids would have a new life there. A fresh start, around people who knew how to look after them.

Gravel crunched under her shoes as she followed Harrison back out to the car. The kids would have a new start. But none of the plans Lainie, Harrison and Arlo had made to house them would work. Not with a sixteen-year-old Eric. Hideaway Cove was strange, but somehow Jacqueline knew it wouldn't be letting-kids-live-on-their-own strange.

No. They would need an adult guardian. Or guardians, plural. Mr. and Mrs. Sweets…

Jacqueline grimaced. The idea of the sweet, enthusiastic Weaver kids under the influence of Mrs. Sweets and her sweetly acidic tongue was enough to make her break out in hives. If only—

She shook her head. Hideaway looked after its own, that's what Arlo said. And Eric and the Wheelers were Hideaway's own, now. The Sweets might be sour assholes to anyone who wasn't a shifter, but Arlo didn't seem any the worse for wear for having the Sweets look after him when he was younger.

And she wasn't going back, anyway.

***

The house seemed bigger than ever.

It had grown like this once before. Right after Derek left. Jacqueline had left the lawyer's office in a daze, driven home, and found herself in a house that didn't fit properly. The rooms were too big and there were too many of them. There had always been too many of them, ever since she found out she couldn't have kids, but she hadn't been prepared for it to be just her, rattling around in the place she'd planned to build so many memories in.

And now it was just her again.

Jacqueline jumped as though she'd stood on a thumbtack. She started moving. She *had* to move, she knew, before the thread of regret she was tugging on like a loose thread unwound her entire life.

She had to move. And the house was empty, and there was nothing else to do, so she cleaned.

Jacqueline dusted. Scrubbed. Mopped. Swept the ceilings and light fixtures and then mopped again because of all the dust that fell down. Scrubbed more things until she realized she was scrubbing the outsides of her kitchen storage tins and rearranged them instead. Then the cutlery drawer. Then the china she only took out when her in-laws came over and why did she even still have it when she hadn't had in-laws in three years? Back in the cabinet.

Or she could throw it all out.

She paused, and that was a bad idea. *Moving good. Stopping bad.* She left the good china where it was and headed for the bathroom.

By the time she'd run out of house to clean, it was getting dark. She stood in the front hall, panting.

Moving good, stopping bad. Except when she was exhausted enough that stopping meant falling asleep, not just sitting gnawing over everything that she'd done wrong in her life.

She should shower. Eat something. Go to bed, wake up, go to work... oh, shit, she still needed to call a tow truck to pick up her poor car...

Jacqueline closed her eyes and leaned back against the front door. Her fresh start was going to have to wait a bit longer. She couldn't even bear to think about her old plans now. Parties. Cocktails. Sexy one-night stands...

She winced.

The first time she'd come home like this, to a suddenly too-big, too-empty house, she'd wanted to rage. To smash all the evidence of the way she'd hoped her life would go until it was all in as many pieces as her heart was.

She'd pushed the anger back, folded it small and tight and put it away where she couldn't feel it anymore.

But this time, there wasn't any anger. Damn it, she was ready for some anger now, some break-shit-now juvenile impulses, because she was done with this house, this town, all her *stuff*, she was going to throw it out anyway and repaint the walls realtor-friendly white and—

And she just felt small, and tired. And very, very alone.

She'd been so close to having, not everything she'd ever dreamed off, but things she'd never dreamed of at all.

Being with Arlo would have been… She didn't have the words to describe it. Magical wasn't enough, because magic made her think of flighty, floaty things, and Arlo was so real it took her breath away. If they stayed together, she could have seen the Weaver kids settle in Hideaway Cove and watched them grow up—making sure they had time to be kids, first.

Instead…

She groaned. "There you go," she murmured to herself. "Moping again. Shouldn't have stopped to think about it…"

She was about to step away from the door when someone knocked on the other side.

CHAPTER EIGHTEEN
Arlo

*H*e knew before the car even came into view that Jacqueline wasn't in it.

The Sweets had left soon after Jacqueline and Harrison. Lainie had muttered something about them not having any reason to stay now they'd done their dirty work, and Arlo...

Arlo shook his head. There was some sort of misunderstanding. There had to be. Ma and Pa were the way they were because they wanted the best for Hideaway Cove. Because they wanted the best for *shifters*.

Didn't they?

He stood in front of Harrison and Lainie's house and watched the Land Rover crest the far hill and wind down the road towards town.

It was mid-afternoon and the streets were busy, at least, busy for Hideaway. People turned towards the car as it drove past. Arlo was too far away to see their faces, but their interest was obvious. A newcomer in Hideaway was always exciting news.

Arlo frowned. *Eric. No last name. Who is he? Some irresponsible oaf who left the kids to fend for themselves when they needed him most. And now he's going to get a hero's welcome in Hideaway, and Jacqueline...*

His heart ached. Jacqueline was gone, fleeing Hideaway as fast as she could, and he had no idea what had gone wrong or how to get her back.

"Arlo?" Kenna poked her head around the door. "What's going on? Where did Jacqueline go? Ms. Eaves wouldn't—"

Her eyes widened and excitement and relief rolled off her in waves. "Eric! That's Eric! Dylan, Tally, Eric's back!"

Arlo bit back a growl of frustration.

Dylan cannonballed out the front door, skidding on the path as he raced over to Arlo.

Lainie was right on his heels, Tally crowing in her arms. "Kenna, I told you not to bother Arlo right now," she began, but broke off when Tally abruptly shifted. "Oh, bother," she gasped, fumbling to keep from dropping the seal pup.

Arlo braced himself. Tally's psychic voice was louder when she was in seal form, and this close, any strong emotion would feel like he'd taken an anvil to the back of his head.

But Tally's joy didn't hit him like a ton of bricks. Instead, he felt buoyant, as though her happiness was lifting him up. Her human and seal emotions swirled together with a single thought at the center:

Pack!

He shut his eyes briefly. Of course Eric was the kids' pack.

He hung back as the Land Rover wove its way up Lighthouse hill. The air was thick with the Weaver kids' joy, and if he stayed too close to them, he thought he might choke on it. They deserved better than that. He wouldn't ruin their alpha's homecoming with his own bitterness. Eric might be a pathetic pack leader, but there would be others to make sure the kids had everything they wanted here in Hideaway without breaking those pack bonds.

Unless this Eric, whoever he was, wanted to start anything. Arlo's wolf

153

bristled. If Eric wanted to have words about how Arlo had stepped into his place these last few days...

The Land Rover growled to a halt in front of the gathered kids. The passenger door burst open, and any thoughts Arlo had had about telling Eric exactly what he thought of a shifter who left his pack alone evaporated.

He's just a kid!

Eric half-stumbled getting out of the car. He was better at keeping his emotions private than the Weaver kids, but Arlo still caught the edge of his bone-crushing relief as they all screamed and leaped on him.

"Eric! Where have you *been*!"

"We went on a boat!"

"We found Hideaway Cove, it's really *real*, you were right—"

"Ahhhhhhh!" Tally screeched happily. *AHHHHH*HHHHHHHHH!*

Eric hugged each of them in turn and straightened, his eyes shining. "I can't believe you're all here. Mr. Galway told me—"

Standing, he topped Kenna by more than a foot. He caught sight of Arlo over her head. Even ten feet away, Arlo could see him gulp.

A heavy weight settled over Arlo's shoulders as he watched the young man pull himself together.

He's just a kid, Arlo thought again. *Look at him now. Gathering his courage to come talk to me. Trying to do the right thing.*

He crossed his arms as Eric approached him, then thought better and put his hands in his pockets. Unthreatening and open.

He's trying to do the right thing. The least I can do is not terrify the pants off him.

"Mr. Hammond?" Eric asked, his voice cracking at the end. He stopped, looking horrified, and cleared his throat before he started again. "Mr. Hammond. Sir. I'm Eric Potts. Mr. Galway said you got the others from the marine reserve and brought them here."

"That's right. It's good to finally meet you."

Eric looked thrown by that. "I, um, thank you. For looking after them.

154

You and Ms. March. I wasn't even sure we were in the right place…"

"You were close enough. We just stepped in to get you the rest of the way."

Arlo held out his hand and Eric shook it, eyes wide. His grip was firm, but the next breath he took was so heavy he rocked back on his feet.

"I've got experience working in shipyards, and on boats. I can fish and I can fix an engine, sometimes, if I know what's wrong with it. And nets. I'll do about anything, I don't mind—"

"Hang on, hang on. I don't need your whole resume." Arlo raised his hands and frowned. "Why are you telling me this?"

"I need a job." Eric looked as confused as Arlo felt. "I don't mind what it is. I don't even need pay, just somewhere for the kids to stay, and food. I'll do anything."

Arlo stared at him. There was something flickering behind his dark eyes. Arlo's wolf pricked its ears up and the flickering stopped, as though Eric's animal had noticed it was being watched.

His wolf barked softly and Eric blinked. "Uh, hello as well to your, um, to…"

"I'm a wolf shifter," Arlo explained.

"Woah."

"And you don't need to get a job. How old are you?"

"Ninet—Uh, eigh… seventeen?" He drew himself up. "You gotta understand. I said I'd look after them. I know we're not the same shifters, but I made a promise. We're in this together."

"They're your pack." Arlo nodded.

"I dunno? We're each other's pack. We don't…" Eric's shoulders slumped. "It's just us."

Arlo sighed. He looked up and caught Harrison's eye. *You hear all that?* he sent to him.

Yep.

"Right." Arlo looked Eric in the eye, then swept his gaze over the three

Weaver kids as well, including them in the conversation. "I know we talked about getting you your own place, but that's out of the question. You've done a good job of looking after yourselves up until now, and it's time for the adults to take over."

"We're not going into some sort of home again!" Kenna blurted out, grabbing Dylan's hand.

"No, you're not," Arlo agreed. "Not some sort of home. Someone's home, and it'll be your home, too."

Kenna exchanged a look with Dylan and Eric. Arlo felt a whisper of their telepathic conversation against the edge of his own consciousness.

"Might have been easier if you told us all this earlier," Harrison pointed out calmly.

Arlo nodded. If they'd known when the Sweets were still here—

His ribs tightened, so hard and so quickly pain shot through his chest. *If I hadn't blown up over Eric, if I'd known that he was just a kid like the others, if I hadn't let my mouth run and driven Jacqueline off...*

Then the kids would be safe in their new home with the Sweets, and Jacqueline would still be here.

Arlo's wolf whined, and he frowned. Something about that picture still didn't fit.

"Harrison's right," he said, making sure to keep his own confusion out of his voice. "If we'd known sooner Eric wasn't old enough to be your guardian, we could have planned things a bit better."

"Well maybe we had our own plans!" Kenna blurted out. She slapped her hands over her mouth, eyes wide, and then let them from. Her head dropped. "Not that that matters, now..."

Arlo shook his head, confused, until he caught the edge of another silent conversation between Kenna and Eric.

...him and Jacqueline...

Arlo stepped away. He didn't want to hear any more, and he didn't want the kids to see his face.

He'd hurt the one woman he was meant to protect with his life. Hurt her so badly she couldn't bear the sight of him. And he didn't even know how.

He closed his eyes. Now that he wasn't worked up over the bogeyman failed-alpha Eric he'd built up in his head out of nothing, maybe he could see beyond his own frustration. Ma Sweets had been talking about pack. That was what had set him off, and—

God. That's what had set Jacqueline off, as well.

Snippets of images and conversations clicked together in his mind. The picture they formed made his heart ache.

Jacqueline's failed marriage. The sliver of ice in her voice when she said there was no one waiting at home for her. The way she'd talked around the fact her ex had gotten another woman pregnant, and what that meant.

And he'd told her the one thing he'd always wanted most in the world was a pack of his own.

Christ. How could I be so blind?

"I have to go," he announced. Everyone's attention was instantly on him. A flicker of satisfaction passed across Harrison's face.

"Keys?" Harrison tossed them over and Arlo caught them without looking. He had already turned to the kids.

He met each of their eyes in turn, and couldn't tell whether the anxious anticipation shivering across his skin was his, or theirs.

"Wait here," he told them. "I've got to fix something. And then I'll be back."

He swallowed. He could tell they wanted him to say more—but he couldn't. He wasn't going to make any promises he couldn't keep.

"Harrison, Lainie, can you look after them? I don't know how long—"

"As long as you need," Harrison said firmly, and Lainie nodded, taking his hand.

Arlo couldn't speak. His whole being was wound tight with the need to go, to fix what he'd broken. If he could. God, he hoped he could.

The Land Rover's engine roared and he drove off to find the other half of his heart.

CHAPTER NINETEEN
Jacqueline

Jacqueline opened the door. Too quickly. She wasn't prepared for who was on the other side, and then there was no time to control her reaction.

"You!" she exclaimed. "What the hell are you doing here?"

Derek gave an easy smile. "Jacqueline."

Jacqueline froze. That smile, those crisp light-blue eyes and the equally un-crisp collars on his shirt—how many times had she asked him to hang his clothes up instead of throwing them on the floor after she'd ironed them...

She shook herself. "Why are you here?" she repeated.

"Can we talk? Inside?" He shot her that smile again and tried to get past her. She stepped in front of him. "Come on, Jacqueline. It's been years. You can't keep me out of my own house."

"It's not your house," she said automatically. "You gave it to me in the settlement. Remember?"

"Well, yeah..." He leaned back, hands on his hips as he looked up at the house. "It's just got so many memories, you know?"

I know.

"So, you gonna let me in?"

"Why were you at the Spring Fling?"

Derek eyeballed her. "Why weren't you? You always used to love that sort of rubbish."

Jacqueline's spine went wobbly. *He was looking for me?* She was instantly suspicious.

"Come on, Jackie," Derek said, smiling. "Let me inside. There's something I want to talk with you about."

"Oh, *now* you want to talk?" Jacqueline couldn't believe what she was hearing.

"Here we go again." Derek turned away, but not so quickly she missed him rolling his eyes.

"What do you mean, again?" The wobbliness in Jacqueline's spine grew prickles. "We've never talked about what happened. I never even got a chance to tell you how you made me feel! I—oh, shit, no."

Another car pulled up on the other side of the street. One she recognized. God, it would be too much to hope it was Harrison or Lainie, wouldn't it? It was their car after all—but—

Arlo stepped out of the driver's seat and the bottom fell out of Jacqueline's stomach.

I can't believe this is happening. I'm going to face off with the man who divorced me because I can't have kids... and the man whose heart I'm going to break for the same reason.

CHAPTER TWENTY
Arlo

The hair on the back of Arlo's neck prickled. He sensed where Jacqueline was even before he saw her, a dark shape in the doorframe, silhouetted by the light inside.

There was a man on the step in front of her.

Arlo crossed the street in a few long strides. "Is this man bothering you, Jacqueline?"

Jacqueline's face was tense. Her hair was tied back, but she gestured as though she was pushing it off her face anyway. "Arlo, now's—"

"I'm not bothering her. I'm her ex-husband. Who the hell are you?"

"I'm—" *Her mate.* The word twisted on his tongue. He wanted it to be true, but he couldn't say it, and not just because the scowling man in front of him wasn't a shifter.

If Jacqueline rejected him, all the words in the world wouldn't make it true.

He stared at Jacqueline imploringly. Her eyes softened, just for a moment, and then went sharp with a pain that cut straight through his chest.

"Arlo's a—a friend," she said.

Thank you, Arlo thought. He knew some people might find being called a "friend" a slap in the face, but for him, it was a bright light of hope.

Maybe he still had a chance to make things right.

"Sure, fine, whatever." Jacqueline's ex—Derek, he remembered now—turned back to Jacqueline. "Look, this is getting ridiculous. Tell your friend to come back another time. What I've got to say is important."

Arlo's hackles rose. His wolf was growling, and it was all he could do to keep himself from growling, too.

Jacqueline made an exasperated noise. "Right. *This* is important."

"That's what I said." Derek jerked his chin towards the street. "Go on, you heard her. This isn't a good time for an impromptu visit."

"Oh, for—do you even hear yourself?"

Derek started forward and found Jacqueline standing in front of him, with her feet planted and her arms crossed.

"Get out of the way, Jackie," Derek said, his voice dripping patience.

Arlo stepped forward. If this man thought he could speak to Jacqueline that way in her own house—

"I'm not letting you in, Derek. I said that already. You just didn't listen. You never—" Jacqueline pressed the heels of her hands against her eyes. "I need to—to talk to Arlo. *That's* important. Whatever you're here for can wait."

Derek spluttered. Jacqueline ignored him and held the door for Arlo.

Arlo's nose wrinkled as he went inside. The house smelled strongly of disinfectant, but it wasn't just that.

He couldn't sense Jacqueline's touch anywhere.

It was a nice house, what he could see of it. Clean neutral carpets, walls papered with some sort of tiny flower pattern. Framed pictures with watercolors of other, bigger flowers. Halfway down the hall was an end-table covered in the sort of knick-knacks that Mrs. Hanson at the bed-and-breakfast loved to collect.

It was nice. But fussy. Which wasn't a word he associated with Jacqueline. "Arlo."

The front door clicked shut, with Derek on the other side of it. Jacqueline sighed and Arlo heard the weight of years of unhappiness in it.

She was wearing the same borrowed shirt and jeans she'd left Hideaway Cove in, but they were dirty. The front of her shirt was patchy with sweat. Arlo ached to hold her.

"I'm sorry about Derek," she said. "He's... well. I don't know if it's tenacity or what it is, but odds are he'll have convinced himself in ten minutes that I don't know what I'm talking about and obviously I meant to let him in, not you."

She paused, clicked her fingers and turned back to the door. Arlo heard the lock turn.

"That should buy us some time," she muttered.

She didn't turn back. Arlo watched her shoulders rise and fall as she took a deep breath.

"Let me start," he said, and she raised her hands.

"No. I need to say this." She turned around and lifted her eyes to meet his. "You want a pack. A—a family. And I can't have kids."

"I know."

Her eyes widened and Arlo reached out to touch her shoulder. She leaned into his touch, so subtly he wondered if she knew she was doing it.

"I put it all together after you left. I'm so sorry for what I said, Jacqueline. God, I was so twisted up in my own past I didn't even think how that might sound." *Please believe me,* he added silently. "You're my pack. You're everything I need."

Jacqueline shook her head, her eyes closed. "We both know that's not true. You want a pack. A *real* family."

"I want *you.*"

She went on as though she couldn't hear him.

163

"And I can't give you any of that! I tried, Derek and I tried for so long, and it didn't work. There's something—"

She gestured painfully towards her midriff. Her mouth rounded.

Arlo grabbed her hand. He could see what word she was about to say, and he couldn't let her say it.

"There's nothing wrong with you."

Jacqueline grimaced. "Come on. That's obviously not—"

"Jacqueline." Arlo wrapped his hands around both of hers and held them to his heart. "You're perfect. You're *everything*. The only pack I need is you. Now or ever."

Jacqueline gulped. "You say that now. But I know how this works. You want a family, and I can't give it to you. You'll—you'll end up resenting me. I don't want to go through that again. I know it's selfish, but I can't. Not again."

Her voice was shaking. Arlo could see how every word hurt her to say.

And he understood.

"Part of that is true. I have always wanted a pack," he said. Jacqueline's eyes locked on to his, bone-dry and wary, as though she was bracing herself for him to give in and agree with her. Well, that wasn't going to happen. "A pack of my own. To cherish and care for. To dedicate my life to. Because the pack I was born into never did that for me."

"But you said—" Jacqueline hesitated, and he willed her to keep going. "Shifters always look after their own."

"Mine didn't." Arlo's voice dropped as he pulled up memories he'd kept hidden deep. How could he put into words things he'd never let himself think about? He felt like he was paddling over black water. Floundering. "My first pack abandoned me after my mother died."

"Oh, God, Arlo."

Jacqueline rushed forward and wrapped her arms around him. Arlo let out a ragged breath. She was a lifeline in the dark, holding him safe above the murky waters.

164

"I traveled around by myself for a while. I was a few years older than Kenna, and I could grow a beard by then, so people either thought I was older than I was, or they didn't care. I did odd jobs. Never stayed in one place long. I didn't fit anywhere, and I didn't know how to make myself fit. Losing my pack was like…"

His stomach lurched at the memory. Jacqueline shivered against him.

"I can't imagine," she whispered. "But the Weaver kids are their own pack, aren't they? And they went through so much to stick together. If they lost each other…"

"It would tear them to pieces."

Arlo's wolf whined. Another memory surfaced: Tally, screaming her head off until she saw Arlo and Jacqueline. The memory tugged at something inside him.

"But you found a place eventually, didn't you? Hideaway Cove. And the Sweets took you in."

"Right…" Arlo frowned. "I found a new pack. And they…"

He shook his head. "The point is, I've lost, too. I know how terrifying it can be to try and find something again that's been snatched away from you. But you *can* find it again. Jacqueline, I won't be like Derek. I won't resent you. I couldn't."

"But a pack—"

"A pack can be two people. Together. In love."

Jacqueline was still holding him close. She tipped her head back to look into his eyes and he lowered his until their foreheads just touched.

"I want that with you. Us. Together. Sailing off into the sunset."

CHAPTER TWENTY-ONE
Jacqueline

I want to believe him. Oh, God, I do.

Jacqueline felt as though her heart was going to rip itself in two. Arlo was saying everything she wanted to hear, everything she *needed* to hear, and she knew deep in her soul that he wouldn't lie to her.

So why was she still so hesitant?

I'm afraid. I'm still so afraid of everything going wrong. I've been afraid all this time. All my plans to go wild, party hard… I never wanted any of that. I was just afraid to admit what I really wanted.

Someone who loves me just the way I am.

"Sailing off into the sunset," she whispered.

"I know we missed tonight's," Arlo said, his words like kisses along the edges of her lips. "But there'll be more."

"Promise?" Jacqueline couldn't keep the hint of anxiety from her voice.

"I promise."

She drew a slow breath. "Derek wasn't the only one who wanted kids. I know it's hypocritical, after what I said about being afraid of you resenting me, but you have to know… I always dreamed of having a house full of kids. It's why we bought this place. But it never happened, and it's never going to happen. I'm sad about that. I'm likely to stay sad about it."

"I understand."

Of course he does, Jacqueline thought, staring up into his eyes. This strong mountain of a man, salt-crusted and calloused and warm and caring. Of course he understood.

"I'm still scared," she admitted, "I…"

I wanted a fresh start.

That's the one thing I told myself that was actually true. And now here it is.

Jacqueline raised her head. Arlo lifted his, his expression confused until he looked into her eyes.

"I'm scared," she said. "Because I don't want to lose you. But that isn't a good enough reason to run away. Just like it wasn't a good enough reason to lock myself up here in Dunston, barely living my life and not even admitting to myself what I wanted."

She took his hand, winding her fingers around his. His hand was so big and strong, practically dwarfing hers, and yet they fit together perfectly. How had she never noticed this before?

"Arlo," she said, and her voice wasn't shaking anymore. "You're my pack."

The noise he made was all she needed to know she'd made the right decision.

"And you're mine," he growled.

Jacqueline pulled him down for a kiss that made her whole body heat up. Their teeth clashed together and she pulled back at the same time he did, and the half-second they each spent checking the other was all right was too much. She kissed him again, hot and passionate, her fingers digging into his scalp.

The same throb of unexpected desire as she'd felt the night before hit her like a train. And this time, she had no desire to slow down. Jacqueline bit down on Arlo's lip and felt him groan, the reverberation coming through his chest and diving straight down between her legs. She was going to ride this need to exhaustion.

There was a knock at the door.

"No…" Jacqueline groaned. "Shoot. I forgot about Derek."

Arlo kissed her neck and then growled against it: "Keep forgetting him."

"What, just leave him out there listening in?" Jacqueline reluctantly unwound herself from Arlo. "I'll get rid of him. Quickly," she reassured him. "*Very* quickly."

She kept hold of Arlo's hand as she unlocked the door. He moved behind the door where he'd be out of sight when she opened it, and a thrill of excitement rippled through her.

"If you need me to make him back off…" Arlo said, and she shook her head.

"I can handle this. It's about time I did."

She opened the door.

"Finally," Derek sighed before she'd even let go of the door handle. "Come on. I've given you time to talk to whoever-he-is. I've got things to do this evening, I can't wait around after you forever."

"And yet here you are. Hanging on my doorstep." Jacqueline put her free hand on her hip. The other one was still holding Arlo's. "Besides. There's something I want to say to you, as well."

She closed her eyes and took a deep breath. This was her chance. For the first time, she felt strong enough to give Derek the tongue-lashing he deserved. To really make him *feel* what he'd done to her.

She tightened her grip on Arlo's hand—and the feeling went away.

Derek was never going to change. He was never going to admit that a version of the world in which he wasn't perfectly justified in everything he did existed. All the time and energy she spent thinking of ways to convince him otherwise were just… time and energy spent thinking about him. And he didn't deserve that.

She wanted a fresh start. Whatever that meant.

And he was holding her back.

Jacqueline opened her eyes.

"Here we go," Derek muttered. He glanced over his shoulder with a furtive look and Jacqueline bit back a groan. There was a car parked further down the street. She could just make out a figure in the passenger seat.

"You know what? I was wrong," she said, and his expression brightened. "I don't have anything to say to you. Have a good life. You and your family. Do a better job of it with them than we managed."

And maybe don't leave them in the car while you go to chat to your ex-wife! she added silently.

"I am," Derek said firmly. "That's why I want the house."

Jacqueline froze.

God damn it.

"Really."

Derek drove on. Jacqueline's ears were buzzing too loudly for her to hear him.

A breath whispered in her ear. "One of those odd jobs I did was guard dog. Just say the word."

Arlo's voice drove away the buzzing and the hollow feeling inside her was replaced by certainty.

"You know, that's handy," she said, grinning. "Because I'm thinking of selling."

"Great!" Derek's whole posture changed as his eyes lit up. "A private sale would be best, you know. I have some options here." He dug around in his coat pocket.

Jacqueline shook her head. "I don't believe it."

"What?"

"You're trying this again? You actually—" She pinched the bridge of her nose. *Being the bigger person is a lot easier when the smaller person doesn't keep trying to kick you in the face.* "Show me those." She snatched the papers from him. "Are you kidding me? This is what the house was worth

169

when we *bought* it."

"The market—"

"Has gone up!" Jacqueline thrust the papers back at him. "Go away, Derek. If you're that desperate for this old place, you can bid at auction like everyone else. And—no, I'm not finished. I meant what I said. I hope you have a good life. But I'm done with you. Don't come back here again."

"Aw, come on, Jackie—"

"Good *bye*, Derek."

She shut the door on his face. Locked it. And threw the bolt, too, for good measure.

"Oh my *God*," she breathed. "I cannot believe I spent ten years of my life with him. No wonder I never want to make a fuss. He just slithers all over any argument like it doesn't exist."

"Jacqueline." Arlo's voice was a low rumble, tinged with an intensity that made her heart sing.

"I know. I'm going to stop talking about him, right now."

"No, I meant… you're going to sell the house?"

The sound of a car starting up and driving away filtered through the door. Jacqueline walked through to the kitchen, pulling Arlo with her.

"As soon as I can. I've put it off too long. I need to get out of Dunston, and I want…" She leaned against a countertop and met his eyes. "We're pack, aren't we? Pack should stick together and there's no way in hell I'm going to make you move to Dunston."

"You'd move to Hideaway?"

"Yes."

Arlo slipped his arms around her waist. His touch sent rivulets of desire through her veins, pooling deep inside her.

"But first…" she added and watched anticipation build in his dark eyes. "Let's finish what we started back there."

Arlo pushed her against the counter, his fingers digging into her waist as he kissed her. Jacqueline bit down gently on his lower lip, making him groan.

She let herself fall back over the counter, forcing Arlo to lean forward, covering her body. His hips were heavy against hers, his cock thick and hard against her stomach.

Need blazed inside her. "Arlo," she said urgently, "I don't think I'll be able to stand it if you take things slow this time."

Arlo growled something she couldn't make out and kissed down her neck to her collarbone. His stubble grazed her sensitive skin.

"Good," he rumbled, and Jacqueline's whole body clenched.

Arlo pushed her shirt up. The first touch of his fingers on her skin drove her mad. Jacqueline tugged it the rest of the way off and he buried his face between her breasts. One of his hands slid into her pants. Jacqueline jerked her hips, urging him further.

"Oh-h, God, yes," she gasped as his fingers slipped between her folds. She was so wet for him already.

"I need you." Arlo kneeled down, undoing her jeans. "When you left—"

His voice was raw. Jacqueline's heart ached, cooling the red-hot desire inside her. She was about to drop to her knees with him when he pulled her jeans and panties down and kissed between her legs.

The rush of pleasure was so intense it left Jacqueline dizzy. Then Arlo's tongue flicked out and it was all she could do not to scream.

Then he slid one finger inside her, and two, and she did scream.

"That's—" Jacqueline gasped, panting as her body shuddered around Arlo's fingers. His tongue flicked out again, teasing her already-sensitized clit, and she moaned. "That's... not fair..."

Arlo kissed his way back up her body. She swayed against him. Her orgasm was still sending aftershocks through her body, but one look at the expression in his eyes made her almost cry out with need again.

"I won't be able to go as slow this time," he said, cupping her face. "If I hurt you—"

"You won't," she gasped, and kissed him. "Please. Now."

171

He moaned deep in his throat, his breath hot against her neck. "I need you," he groaned.

She understood. He wanted the same thing she did. Hard and fast, burning away the misery that had separated them.

She tugged at his pants. He was already rock hard, and she ran her hands down his length, shivering in anticipation. Going slow had been intense enough—going fast…

She sat back up on the counter and kicked her jeans off. Arlo closed the space between them, his eyes dark as sin. He kissed her, claiming her mouth with a passion that left her breathless, and thrust inside her in one strong movement.

"Oh God!" Jacqueline cried out. "Please. More!"

She needed him with an intensity that made her whole body ache.

He filled her, hard and deep, each thrust driving more pleasure from her singing nerves until she felt like she was dissolving with ecstasy. It didn't hurt. It was just pleasure, her body yearning for his masculine power as he filled her again and again. His energy was almost animalistic, frenzied, but his eyes were full of the same warm, steady love as ever. He just needed her, as desperately as she needed him.

She wrapped her legs around his waist and pulled him closer, so every driving thrust brought him fully inside her. He groaned into her shoulder, his own body stiffening as he came closer to climax, and the knowledge that *she* was doing this to him, that her body was bringing him so much pleasure his eyes were ragged with it, sent her over the edge again.

"Oh, God! Oh, Arlo, I—"

Jacqueline's hand slipped, and something crashed to the floor.

"Oh, for the love of—" she panted. Arlo paused. "No, don't stop!"

He drove into her again, holding her close to his chest. She was dizzy with joy, and when Arlo came his climax was so intense it left them both breathless.

They clung together, panting. After a few minutes Arlo raised his head and looked over her shoulder.

"I'm sorry. That was a vase. Should have been more careful." Despite his words, his expression was utterly at peace.

"Don't be sorry. And don't be careful. I hate all this junk." She kissed him and grinned. "It's all rubbish the in-laws gifted us. Should have thrown it all out years ago."

"In that case..." Arlo hoisted her up again and made a slow circuit of the kitchen. Jacqueline cackled with laughter as her feet knocked knick-knacks off the counters. She made an especially dramatic swipe when she got to the rooster-shaped paper-towel-holder and couldn't help cackling at it crashed to the floor.

"Where to next?" Arlo asked, nuzzling her neck.

"The bathroom." Jacqueline nipped at his ear.

"You want to clean up?"

The light in his eyes made her skin thrill. *Again?* she thought silently. *Already?*

She narrowed her eyes. "After I've smashed one more thing."

When they got to the bathroom, she booted the be-doiley'd toilet roll doll off the vanity. It hit the mirror and bounced out the window, trailing toilet paper.

"Oops," she said unrepentantly, and swiped one foot across the decorative soaps. "Hah!"

"Why do you have all this stuff?" Arlo asked.

Jacqueline surveyed the mess. "You might as well ask, why have this house? I've been so *stuck*. I stuck here paying the mortgage because I thought it was the right thing to do, I stuck with all the furniture we got for wedding gifts because I thought it was more sensible than buying new... It's all leftovers. From another life." She grinned. "And now that I'm finally selling up, smashing it all now is the last chance I'll have to get any real use out of them."

Arlo's eyes shone. "Want me to carry you around any other rooms?"

"Maybe later. Right now, I want to soap you up."

She thought, as she watched hot water streaming over Arlo's chest, that maybe she'd found her equilibrium again and they'd go back to the slow, sensuous pace they'd had that night on the boat. A few minutes later, panting for breath as Arlo kneeled between her legs, she realized she was wrong. And started to wonder whether they'd ever be able to slow down again.

"Right," Arlo said after they'd each washed up a second time. His eyes were sparkling. "Which way to the bedroom?"

Jacqueline directed him down the hall, kicking figurines and paper flowers off end tables as she went. It took them a while to reach the bedroom, as now that she'd started violently dismantling her old life, she didn't want to stop.

Luckily Arlo didn't seem to see anything unusual about the fact that her route to the bedroom took them through the kitchen, the dining room, and the front hall again. She even managed to dislodge one of the miserable sad-kitten pictures someone had given her as a wedding present.

The house was a total mess behind them, and it was *great*.

"Ahh," she sighed as Arlo carefully put her down on the bed. "That feels good."

Arlo lay down beside her. She rolled on top of him automatically, planting her elbows either side of his head.

"Thank you," she said. "For chasing after me and making me see reason."

"Thank you for giving me another chance."

She stroked his cheek. "I spent so long chasing a dream I couldn't have. I forgot that sometimes dreams do come true."

She'd come so close to giving up, to letting her pain twist her up until she couldn't see how many wonderful things the universe had left in it.

Even if she would never have the home full of children she'd longed for…

A shadow of concern passed over Arlo's face.

174

"What is it?" she asked.

"Just a thought." Arlo pulled her down to kiss her. "About dreams."

"A good thought?"

"I think so." He rolled over until they were lying side by side and combed his fingers through her hair. "I have an idea…"

He whispered it to her and she covered her mouth, barely daring to believe what she'd just heard. "Really?"

"Really."

"You think it'll work?"

"If I know Hideaway Cove, it will."

Jacqueline kissed him, joy singing in her veins.

Maybe dreams can come true, after all. All of them.

CHAPTER TWENTY-TWO
Arlo

Jacqueline woke up first; Arlo drifted into wakefulness with the same slight unease he always had waking up on solid land, and then heard her moving elsewhere in the house.

Something that sounded like china shattered, and Jacqueline's laughter drove away any trace of landsickness.

Arlo sat up. The bed creaked.

"Arlo?" There was the sound of footsteps, and then Jacqueline poked her head around the door. "I was going to make pancakes but, er, it just occurred to me that I smashed my only mixing bowl last night..."

Arlo frowned, going over her parade of destruction. "The one with the ducklings on it?"

"Ugh, yes." Jacqueline grinned and smoothed down her shirt. To Arlo's slight disappointment, she was wearing far more clothes than she'd gone to sleep in. "So I thought we could pick up something on the way."

Arlo's wolf stirred. He jumped up, its excitement firing up his body. "Great idea."

Harrison's truck was a stick shift, and the road to Hideaway wound up, down and around so many bends that Arlo was almost mad with not touching Jacqueline before they were halfway there.

You just spent the night with her! he reminded himself, but it didn't help.

He glanced sideways and caught Jacqueline looking at him. Her lips curved into a smile and she reached over to put a hand on his shoulder.

Arlo hadn't realized he'd been tense, but that simple touch relaxed him better than a whole week at anchor in a sunny bay full of fish. He sighed.

"Am I that obvious?"

"Maybe. Maybe I just want to keep hold of you so I know this is actually happening." Jacqueline whistled out a breath. "You're sure this is going to work?"

"You remember what Ma Sweets said." Arlo's voice became grim when he mentioned his foster mother. "Everyone at Hideaway works together to keep pack together."

"Shifters look after their own." Jacqueline's voice was soft, and sad. Arlo bent his head to kiss her hand where it lay on his shoulder.

"If she wants to keep saying that, then she'll need to play ball," he said.

Or else admit that it's all a lie, and the only people the Sweets look after are themselves.

He tightened his grip on the steering wheel.

"And what about the kids?"

Arlo blew out a long breath. "You already know I'm not good at connecting the dots," he said. "Well, I think I've just figured out one of the other things the kids were keeping on the down-low."

He'd called on Jacqueline's landline before he left, asking Harrison to make sure the kids all knew they were coming back, but Tally's lonely panic was still fresh in his mind. He didn't want to put any of them through that again.

He felt the Weaver kids a mile out from Hideaway and clenched his teeth. It wasn't the skull-busting agony he'd felt the night he sailed in

177

to find Jacqueline diving into the waves, or the pure unhappiness of the morning before. The kids' packlessness throbbed like an old bruise.

Don't worry, he thought, wishing his telepathy reached further. *We're on our way.*

Jacqueline squeezed his shoulder as they crested the rise that swept down to Hideaway Cove. "Can you reach them yet?"

He hadn't said anything about mindspeaking to the kids. Jacqueline was just on the same wavelength as he was. He shook his head. *How did I end up with such a perfect mate?*

"Give it to the ice cream parlor," he said, nodding towards Tess's café. Its windows sparkled in the morning sun. "Wait a minute…"

"Hmm?"

Tess?

Tess's voice hit his mind like a splash of sea spray. *Arlo. Good. Come on down, everyone's here.*

"Strike that," Arlo said to Jacqueline. "They're all at the parlor."

She frowned. "Why? What's going on?"

"One sec." Arlo concentrated. *Kenna? Dylan? Tally?*

The seal shifters' minds sparked at his contact. There was another presence with them: Eric, he guessed. Harrison was there, too, which meant at least whatever else was going on, the kids probably hadn't tried to stage a midnight escape.

He reached further and groaned.

He parked outside the parlor and opened the passenger door for Jacqueline. "The Sweets are here," he warned her.

"Good to know." Jacqueline narrowed her eyes. "Don't worry. Now that I know what their deal is, I can handle them. Besides… I've been connecting some dots of my own. I may just have an ace up my sleeve."

He gave her a questioning look, but she just smiled.

The bell above the door jangled as he pushed it open.

Someone had pushed all the café tables into a square in the middle of the room, and everyone was seated around them. Harrison and Lainie on one side, with Ma and Pa Sweets opposite them. The Weaver kids and Eric were seated facing the door. Kenna had a familiar scowl on her face that melted away when she saw Arlo and Jacqueline, and Dylan jumped up.

"You're here!"

"That we are." Arlo sent them all a wave of support. Eric blinked, taken aback. *Of course. I've only been doing that with the younger kids.*

Then, to his surprise, he felt a tentative telepathic nudge from the teen.

Thanks, Eric said into his mind. *That means a lot. And… I guess Kenna was right about you. She said you'd come back.*

Tess was fussing behind the counter, which left the fourth side of the table free. Arlo pulled out a chair for Jacqueline, feeling Ma Sweets' eyes on him, as he sat down.

"Morning, everyone," Jacqueline said, bright and chirpy. "Did you four sleep okay?"

"Wee-e-e-e-ell—" Dylan began, stretching out the word.

"Did Tally have another nightmare?" Jacqueline reached across the Franken-table and Tally cooed and grabbed her finger.

"Not the *same* nightmare…" Kenna's expression was drifting back towards sullen. Her eyes flicked towards the Sweets.

"What's everyone doing here, anyway?"

Tess stormed out from behind the counter and plonked a tray of hot drinks on the table. "Coffee," she said, at the same moment Lainie muttered: "Neutral ground?"

Arlo met Tess's eyes. *All right, sis?*

She tugged on the cuffs of her long-sleeved shirt. *The usual.*

The problem was, Arlo didn't know what Tess's usual was anymore. Like him, she'd always been proud of Ma and Pa Sweets' strong line on keeping Hideaway Cove safe. But ever since they'd discovered exactly how the Sweets had gone about keeping Hideaway "safe", Tess's relationship with their parents had become strained.

And now Lainie was calling her parlor neutral ground?

He raised one eyebrow at Tess, thinking, but not mindspeaking, *Whose side are you on?* She glared at him and stalked back behind the counter.

"Waffles?" she called out, and everyone in the room under the age of twenty called out some variant of "Yes, please, I'm starving."

Tally's version was more of a high-pitched eagle-screech. Ma Sweets took advantage of the noise to pretend she was brushing a mote of dust off her sleeve, and speak telepathically with Arlo.

I'm glad you're here. You know these children, and you of everyone knows what they need right now. Please, help me talk some sense into your poor friends.

"Why don't you talk out loud, Ma?" Arlo kept his voice light. "There's two of us can't hear a word you're saying if you stick to telepathy."

Ma Sweets frowned. "That was *meant* only for you, Arlo," she said, pursing her lips.

"We're talking about the kids." Arlo nodded to them. "Seems rude to exclude them from the conversation, too."

"*Very well.*" Ma Sweets sniffed. "Dear?"

Pa Sweets shuffled slightly in his seat. "My thoughts exactly, dear," he mumbled, and appeared to fall back asleep. Ma Sweets frowned.

"What Dorothy is failing to say—sorry, Mrs. Sweets, I'm sure you were going to get to it in a minute—is that we caught them this morning convincing the kids they were being sent to live with them." Harrison sounded all good manners and one hundred percent pissed off at the same time.

Arlo exchanged a look with Jacqueline. "I'm glad we didn't leave any later," Jacqueline murmured. Arlo squeezed her hand.

Ma opened her eyes wide. "Well, I don't see what's so bad about—"

"Kidnapping?" Lainie suggested, quick as a whip.

"Now I'm confused." Ma Sweets tapped her pursed lips with one fingertip. "Surely you're not complaining that we're taking children in, now? It's not like we're sending them away. Isn't that what you've had a bee in your bonnet about until now?"

"*Grandma!*"

Tess slammed down a plate on the counter. It cracked in two.

"You're not even pretending anymore?" There was only a hint of pleading in Tess's voice, but it was enough to make Ma Sweets' eyes sharpen.

"Pretend what? That our community isn't disintegrating around us?" She fixed Lainie with a knifelike stare.

Arlo tightened his grip on Jacqueline's hand. *How did it take me so long to see the Sweets for what they really are? I was so desperate for someone to take me in, I never questioned what being part of the Sweets' pack actually meant.*

Ma Sweets spoke slowly, as though she was explaining something to a child. "Seals are group animals. Seal shifters need a pack to thrive. These children have each other, but they're a pack without a leader. Arlo knows how difficult that is, don't you, dear?"

"I do."

"See—"

"But they already have a pack leader." Arlo raised his eyebrows at Jacqueline and she mock-glared at him.

"Two pack leaders," she corrected him, and grinned at the kids. "If they want us."

There was half a second of silence, and then the room exploded with noise.

It was something special, Arlo decided, that all four of the shifter kids met Jacqueline's suggestion with even more enthusiasm than they'd shown for the waffles.

"Yes! *Finally*," Kenna cried out. Dylan threw his head back and whooped. Tally banged her fists on the table, and Eric gave a shy smile.

Arlo braced himself for the wave of unguarded emotion. There was no way he was going to let any of the kids see him wince with the migraine that would no doubt come along with it. But the only thing that hit him was the kids' joy.

His *pack's* joy.

Everything slotted into place. All his headaches had been his body's reaction to him rejecting the truth: that these kids filled a gap in his heart he hadn't let himself admit even existed.

Ma Sweets' eyes narrowed. "Have you really thought this through, Arlo? Where are you going to live? That boat of yours—"

"Lighthouse Hill." Lainie's eye gleamed. "I know the perfect section."

Ma scoffed. "And how do you intend to afford that?"

"I'm selling my house." Jacqueline sounded perfectly calm. "You can help me with that, can't you, Lainie? Arlo tells me you're a realtor."

"That's hardly instant money." Ma leaned back in her seat and sniffed. "What are you going to do until then? Set up camp beds in your workshop? I thought you were more sensible than that, Arlo."

And I thought you actually had shifters' best interests at heart. Arlo ran his fingers through his hair.

"This is Hideaway we're talking about. It's like you always said, Dorothy. Shifters look after their own. Whether that's other shifters, or the non-shifters we need to be whole."

The warmth and love in Jacqueline's face made his soul light up.

His own pack had let him down. The Sweets had let him down, too, tainting the true meaning of pack with their hatred.

But with Jacqueline at his side, that was going to change. Their pack would be what packs were meant to be.

Home.

CHAPTER TWENTY-THREE
Jacqueline

It worked. That was the strangest part. She and Arlo had marched
into the tense confrontation between the Sweets and the other
shifters, declared that, actually, *they* were going to look after the new kids,
thank you very much, and everyone accepted it.

Even Mrs. Sweets had reluctantly agreed to support Arlo's new pack
before she left in a huff. Of course, that might have had something to
do with Jacqueline's ace up her sleeve. She'd put together the pieces and
figured out how Mrs. Sweets knew so much about her that she could
needle Jacqueline with barbs about her infertility.

Bridge. Deirdre must have told the Sweets everything about her. But
Deirdre's gossip was a two-way street, and Jacqueline had spent enough
work days listening to her grumble about the Dorothy and Alan who
won every single bridge tournament they attended. All it had taken was
for Jacqueline to whisper—*sweetly*—in Dorothy Sweets' ear that wouldn't
it be awful if everyone here in Hideaway who thought she was such an
upstanding member of the community—who would never do *anything* to

risk their secret being found out by human outsiders—knew that she was using her shifter powers to cheat at cards, and she'd folded.

Jacqueline wasn't sure if she'd folded because she didn't want her neighbors to know about her cheating, or didn't want them to know she stooped so low as to cheat at a game against *humans*, but either way, the Sweets were going to support Arlo's pack.

Except... it's not Arlo's *new pack. It's mine, too. Ours.*

Tess had timed the waffles perfectly for her parents' exit. Across the table, Tally had wolfed hers down in a second flat. Jacqueline could guess what was coming next.

Tally slithered off her seat and ran under the table to hug Jacqueline's legs. She bit back a smile and then, thinking better of it, let herself laugh out loud.

Perhaps that's the strangest part, actually. Over one weekend, I've gone from being single to finding the love of my life and four children. A family.

She met Arlo's eyes. They were full of a deep, contented happiness that made warmth spread through her entire body.

It was strange, but it was a good strange. She wasn't scared; she was excited. Whatever came next, she was ready to greet it with open arms.

"Up you get," she said, lifting Tally onto her knee. Tally giggled and reached for her half-eaten waffle.

Jacqueline glanced at Arlo. She knew Tally's telepathic shrieks cut through his skull like a hot knife through butter. "Are you all right?" she whispered.

He kissed her hand. "Never better," he said, and slid his plate with an extra waffle along to her.

Never better. He was right. This wasn't the life Jacqueline had planned—it was so much more than that.

Forget two-point-five children and a house in the suburbs with a white picket fence. She had a pack of seals and a sea wolf to sail into the sunset with.

And whatever Eric was. She grinned at him across the table as he spooned ice cream onto his waffles.

"You're all right with all of this?" she asked. "The whole pack thing? We've hardly met yet, and it's a big decision."

He nodded fervently and Kenna answered for him. "Oh my God, yes. He's so sick of having to be in charge."

Eric gave an abashed smile. "Yeah. And it feels right, you know? Like Kenna said…"

"Hey!" Kenna smacked him on the arm. "I haven't told them about that yet!"

"About what?" Arlo asked.

"I think I can guess." Jacqueline put down her fork and carefully pushed the second plate Arlo had given her out of Tally's reach. "You knew from the start that you wanted Arlo to be your pack leader, didn't you?"

She remembered how the three of them had put their heads together and whispered conspiratorially back on the cold, windy beach that night. It felt like an eternity ago.

Kenna blushed. "Maybe."

"And you too!" Dylan burst out. He waved his knife and fork. "But Kenna said we couldn't just *say* that, because you're a human and we might scare you off and then nothing would work, so we had to wait until you fell in love and Eric got back!" He beamed at them and then dove back into his waffles.

"Wait." Jacqueline frowned. "Is that why you kept getting worried when you would argue, or when Tally stole my dinner?"

"I didn't want anything to go wrong!" Kenna blurted out. "I thought, if we didn't behave, you wouldn't want us."

A lump formed in Jacqueline's throat. "Well, stop worrying about that right now."

"That's right," Arlo rumbled. "Pack doesn't mean never fighting, or never disagreeing. It means we're there for you. Always."

185

Kenna dropped her eyes and stabbed her fork into her waffle. "Well, I know that *now*," she muttered.

"Good." Arlo said, and Jacqueline echoed him.

"Because in a few years we'll be a three-teenager household, and if that isn't a recipe for scrapping then I don't know what is," she added.

Arlo raised his eyebrows. "There's a thought." He flashed a grin at Harrison. "We'd better get started on that house."

"And selling mine. Good thing I have a buyer already lined up." Jacqueline narrowed her eyes. "But you have to promise me you'll squeeze him for everything he's worth, Lainie."

"It'll be my pleasure." Lainie pulled her phone out. "Now, about this house. What are you thinking? Open plan? How many bedrooms? The section closest to the water is still available. I'll need to talk to the architect but I had some ideas about over-water rooms…"

"What do you reckon?" Arlo asked the kids. "You'll be living there."

Their faces glowed and they all leaned forward, ideas spilling from their lips.

"Bunk beds—"

"A trapdoor to jump in the water—"

"A REALLY big den—"

"Their plan seems to have all worked out."

Jacqueline looked up to see Tess standing behind her. She smiled at her and Tess smiled back, crookedly.

"What about your plan?" Jacqueline asked, remembering what Tess had said before she ran away from the restaurant during her and Arlo's date.

Tess frowned. "It's… ongoing." Her face cleared. "But I have a good idea of what to do next." She nodded decisively.

"Okay, okay! That's enough ideas for now," Lainie laughed, putting away her phone. "Has everyone had enough to eat?"

There were nods all around. Arlo stood up and offered his arm to Jacqueline.

"I think we need to celebrate," he announced. "Who wants to go for a swim?"

Jacqueline took his arm. "Sounds great," she said.

The morning sun was high in the sky as they all picked their way down the concrete steps from the promenade onto the beach. Sunlight glittered in the waves. Jacqueline hesitated and then, seeing the kids tear their clothes off and run screaming into the water, she stripped down to her t-shirt and undies and tiptoed to the water's edge.

"Ooh, that's cold," she whispered as the waves lapped over her feet.

"As cold as it was on Friday night?" Arlo came up beside her and wrapped one arm around her waist.

"I had other things on my mind then..." Jacqueline shivered and checked on the kids. That bigger seal had to be Kenna, with the tiny seal pup Tally bobbing at her side. Dylan was still in human form, up to his ribcage in the water. As Jacqueline watched, a big gray bird landed on his head, honked, and flapped its wings until Dylan toppled over, laughing.

The goose honked again and dove under the waves as Dylan chased it.

"Is that Eric?" Jacqueline twisted to look back at where she'd last seen the teenaged boy on the beach. "I didn't realize he was a bird—hey!"

Arlo's arm tightened around her waist. "I think he has the right idea," he muttered into her hair, pulling her a step deeper into the water. Icy waves slapped against her shins.

Jacqueline squealed. "Not fair! Ooh, shoot, that's cold..."

She feigned trying to back up, then darted forwards, dragging Arlo with her. When he was balanced on one leg, she struck.

"Argh!" Arlo yelled as she tickled his ribs. He stumbled forward, splashing, and Jacqueline ran into the waves.

She winced as the water passed her thighs, then took a deep breath and dove. The sea enveloped her like an old memory, cold and achy but instantly invigorating. She kicked, remembering how good it felt to swim underwater when she wasn't afraid for her life. Sunlight sparkled through the water, reflecting off a million particles of sand suspended in the waves.

Jacqueline surfaced, gasping with the cold. She trod water, looking around. Kenna and Tally were ganging up on Eric, swimming up underneath him and bumping him out of the water with their heads. Dylan was racing in circles around them.

There was a splash and a rush of breath behind her, and then warm arms wrapped around Jacqueline's waist. Arlo nuzzled her cheek.

"They'll be happy here," he said.

"I know." Jacqueline turned around and kissed him. "Our family. Our pack."

"And you." Arlo cupped her face in his hands and kissed her again, slow and tenderly. "My precious mate. My love. None of this would have happened without you."

Jacqueline wrapped her arms around him and rested her head on his shoulder. The ocean stretched out around them, enveloped by the protective slopes of Hideaway Cove.

She'd been paralyzed with fear for so long, she'd forgotten what it was like to take action and ride the consequences through, whatever happened. But she'd finally done it. Everything could have gone wrong—but instead, it was going so, so right.

She kissed Arlo hard.

I know what I want. And this is it.

Not just a fresh start—a whole new world to explore.

With my mate.

EPILOGUE
Arlo

"*Y*ou'll get it all sweaty!" Kenna chided him.

"Ahh!" Tally added. "Yuck!"

Arlo clenched his fist around the small circle of metal. Kenna tsked at him.

"Give it to me!"

"Give what to you? Arlo, what—"

Jacqueline's voice broke off in a gasp of amazement as she rounded the corner. Arlo spun around, clasping his hands together behind his back. Kenna immediately started prying his fingers apart.

Arlo was too distracted by the sight of his mate to care.

It was three months since Jacqueline had come to Hideaway Cove and Arlo's solitary life had exploded. The bones of their house at the bottom of Lighthouse Hill had been built: a strong foundation for what would soon be the bustling home for their pack, half tucked into the hill, half stretching out over the water. Jacqueline had split her time between Dunston and Hideaway... until now.

Arlo drew in a deep breath. The white button-down shirt he'd borrowed off Harrison scratched at his throat. He'd told Jacqueline he had something important to talk to her about tonight. Had she guessed what he was planning?

She was wearing a flowing dress that made her look like a mermaid who'd just stepped out of the waves. Her hair was held off her face in a tumble of glossy curls. But it was her eyes that shone the brightest as she took in Arlo in his scratchy suit, the four children gathered around, and the covered table behind them.

"What's going on?" she asked, her lips curving into a smile. "Dylan, you said you had a surprise to show me before the party at Caro's?"

She was talking to Dylan, who'd led her in, but her eyes were locked on to Arlo's. He swallowed. Kenna pushed something back into his hands: a small box.

Eric cleared his throat. "We're going to head to Caro's soon. But first…"

They were standing on what would one day be the living room of their pack's home. Right now, it was more like a deck overlooking the water, with tarp-covered stud walls outlining where the walls and doors would one day be. Eric nodded to Kenna and they each expertly flicked the tarps away, revealing strings of glittering fairy lights wound around and between them.

Jacqueline gasped and Arlo's heart swelled. The kids had all made huge strides in their control of their telepathic abilities, but they couldn't keep their pride from leaking out as they watched Jacqueline take in their decorations. They had turned the work site into a magical grotto.

"This is amazing," Jacqueline breathed.

"We're going to head off now." Kenna tossed her head and sent Arlo a telepathic command so brusque and no-nonsense that he couldn't help a sudden bark of laughter. "The Menzies are doing a big sleepover after the party so we'll see you tomorrow, okay?"

She hugged Jacqueline and gestured for the others to all do the same.

Arlo waited as Jacqueline hugged them all goodnight. She picked Tally up for a cuddle and a kiss, before handing her to Kenna.

Jacqueline raised her eyebrows at Arlo as the kids headed back to the main road to walk to the restaurant. "What did Kenna say to you?"

"You noticed that?" Arlo rubbed the back of his neck.

"I'm getting better at picking up on it, I think." Jacqueline slipped up to him and kissed him gently on the lips. Arlo's whole body thrilled.

"I'll tell you after," he promised.

"After…?" Jacqueline was practically glowing. Arlo gestured to the table. "Dinner?"

He held out a chair for her. She sat down, a smile dancing around her lips. When he whipped the cloth off the table, she laughed with delight.

"Since you missed out the first time," Arlo said gruffly.

Dylan had timed Jacqueline's arrival perfectly; the delicate fish and fresh bread were still steaming, making small beads of moisture appear on the chilled bottle of wine. Arlo sat down opposite Jacqueline, hiding the box in his lap.

"Is this what you were doing out on the boat this morning?" Jacqueline asked as he filled her glass.

"Some of it."

"Ooh. Color me intrigued." Jacqueline flashed him a smile that made his skin thrill.

Arlo cut her a slice of bread and buttered it. The butter melted into the warm bread almost immediately. He felt Jacqueline's eyes on him as he added fish to her plate and handed it back to her.

"Thanks," she whispered, her voice warm. "Oh, my God, this is delicious."

"I wasn't going to steal you away from Caro's summer barbeque for bad cooking," Arlo pointed out.

"Good. *Mmm.* I can see why Tally hoovered her way through all of mine that first night."

Arlo watched Jacqueline eat. His heart felt so full, there wasn't room for it in his chest.

How did I get this lucky? he asked himself as they ate, savoring every bite.

"Dessert," he said next. Tess had delivered a batch of specially made ice cream earlier in the afternoon. He pulled it out of the cooler now and Jacqueline cocked one eyebrow.

"From Tess? Should I be worried?"

"She promised no experiments."

Jacqueline closed her eyes as she tasted the ice cream. "Oh!"

Arlo's skin warmed. "Good oh?"

"Yes." Jacqueline opened her eyes and gazed at him. "Here."

She held her spoon to Arlo's lips. He tasted it, not breaking eye contact with her.

"It's the same as the chocolates we had on our first date. Do you remember?"

Thank you, Tess. Arlo sipped his wine.

"I am sensing a theme," Jacqueline said cautiously, her eyes sparkling.

"Don't worry. I haven't arranged for Tally to start screaming in the distance," Arlo joked.

"Thank God."

Arlo let himself sink into Jacqueline's smile. He'd never imagined that having a mate would be like this. Thrilling and easy at the same time.

It was hard for him to think back to what his life had been like before Jacqueline and their pack were in it, but he had to.

"I've been so busy with the house, I haven't been out fishing since the day I met you," he said. "I was miserable then. I didn't even know why. I thought I knew how the world worked and how I fit into it, and everything I learned that told me otherwise hurt. I couldn't even admit to myself what the Sweets were really like."

"Arlo—" Jacqueline reached across the table to take his hand. Arlo folded his fingers around hers.

192

"And then I met you. And everything I thought I knew about the world and how I fit into it turned completely on my head. But it didn't hurt anymore. I finally understood what my own soul had been telling me."

He wrapped both his hands around hers. "Love is more important than fear. Openheartedness is more powerful than defensiveness. I was so scared of losing what I thought was my pack, I didn't realize they *weren't* my pack. You saved me from that. You showed me what love really is."

He took one of his hands away with hers and fumbled with the small box.

"You're the heart of this pack, Jacqueline." He kneeled down on one knee and Jacqueline gasped. "You've thrown yourself into this world with so much courage and so much love it takes my breath away."

"You're the strong one," Jacqueline protested. "You saved my life. You stood up to your parents…"

"I couldn't have done it without you at my side. And in my heart." He took a deep breath. "I know you've done this before and it hasn't worked out. But I need you to know that I'm yours. I want to be bound to you in every way. The mate bond, our pack… and in marriage." He opened the box. "Jacqueline March, will you do me the honor of becoming my wife?"

Jacqueline was completely still. Arlo's heart was in his throat. Then she made a noise that was half-laughter, half-sob, and slid from her chair. "Yes! Of course!"

She threw her arms around his neck and kissed him so hard he almost dropped the ring box. He exclaimed and fumbled for it and she grabbed for it, too, laughing against his lips. At last they both had their hands around it.

"I love you," Jacqueline whispered as he slipped the ring onto her finger. "Marrying you is the only thing I can think of to make our life even more perfect."

Arlo pulled her close against her. They sat together, gazing at the ring in the glittering light of the fairy lights.

"It's beautiful," Jacqueline whispered.

"The kids helped," Arlo said. "Eric came up with the design. Kenna and Dylan chose the stones. And Tally... Tally did a really good job of not swallowing any of the pieces, or anything else in the workshop."

"You made it yourself?" Jacqueline cupped her hand over the ring, treasuring it. But only for a second, before she had to look at it again.

"The guys helped. And the kids. And YouTube."

Jacqueline laughed. "It's perfect."

"It's not." Arlo's voice was rough. "It's—look, you can see where I slipped and took a groove out of the edge. And there's—Tally decided she likes hammers—I think I managed to buff out most of the dent, but you can still see it if you know where to look..."

She kissed him and he shut up.

"Shh. It's perfect. Dents and all."

She held out her hand and the fairy lights shimmered on the gold band with its cluster of tiny stones. The central gemstone was a dark sapphire with glints of lighter color in its heart, like sunlight on deep water. Around it were arranged four smaller London topazes.

"It's the pack," she breathed.

Arlo's heart swelled. Of course she'd understood. "Tally, Dylan, Kenna, Eric... and me," he said. "So you can always keep us close."

Jacqueline curled the fingers of her other hand over her ring and kissed him again. When she pulled away her eyes were shining.

With happiness, Arlo reminded himself as his heart thudded. *She only cries when she's happy.*

"What did Kenna say before she left?" Jacqueline asked.

Arlo rested his forehead against hers. "That I'd better not come find them until you'd agreed to marry me."

Jacqueline burst out laughing. "She didn't! No, God, of course she did." She sighed happily. "I suppose it will make things easier. Making

194

it official, finishing the house—so we square up our little family with the authorities."

Arlo nuzzled her, brushing his lips across the soft skin of her cheekbones. "That's not the reason I'm doing this."

"I know." Jacqueline wiped her eyes. "What now? Back to Caro's?"

Arlo paused. There was a huge celebration waiting for them at Caro's, he was sure.

"There's one more thing I have to show you," he said. "On the boat."

Jacqueline raised her eyebrows. "We've missed sunset again," she pointed out.

Arlo looked up at the stars. "I know."

He rowed Jacqueline out to the *Hometide*. Her eyes were soft and happy, so different to that first time they'd rowed out together.

He helped her up on board and led her down into the cabin. Everything was freshly scrubbed and oiled, and the air smelled faintly of sawdust. Arlo lay Jacqueline down on the bed and propped himself up above her.

"What's doing that?" she asked, touching his face. Arlo raised one hand; colored lights danced over it. Jacqueline's eyes widened as she figured it out.

She rolled over, pushing herself up on her hands and knees to look at the newly repaired port window above the bed.

"Oh, Arlo," she breathed.

He pushed a stray curl behind her ear, letting the joy on her face wash over him.

"I figure with four kids, no matter how good our intentions, we're going to keep missing the real sunsets," he said, his voice rough. "But we'll always have this one."

He'd replaced the broken window with a stained glass picture. The sun, setting over the sea.

"I love it," Jacqueline whispered. She rolled onto her back and pulled him down on top of her, her curves molding to his body. "And I love you."

She kissed him, and Arlo knew: whatever happened next, every day of his life, his love for this woman would grow stronger.

A NOTE FROM ZOE CHANT

Thank you for reading *The Sea Wolf's Mate*! I hope you enjoyed it.

Please consider reviewing *The Wolf's Mate*, even if you only write a line or two. I appreciate all reviews, whether positive or negative.

The cover of *The Sea Wolf's Mate* was designed by Marie Hodgkinson.

ZOE CHANT
COMPLETE BOOK LIST

All of my books are available through Amazon.com.

Check my website, zoechant.com, for my latest releases.

While series should ideally be read in order, all of my books are standalones with happily ever afters and no cliffhangers. This includes books within series.

BOOKS IN SERIES

A Mate for Christmas

Book 1: A Mate for the Christmas Dragon

Book 2: *Christmas Hellhound*

Book 3: *Christmas Pegasus*

Bears of Pinerock County

Book 1: *Sheriff Bear*

Book 2: *Bad Boy Bear*

Book 3: *Alpha Rancher Bear*

Book 4: *Mountain Guardian Bear*

Book 5: *Hired Bear*

Book 6: *A Pinerock Bear Christmas*

Bodyguard Shifters

Book 1: Bearista

Book 2: Pet Rescue Panther

Book 3: Bear in a Bookshop

Book 4: Day Care Dragon

Book 5: Bull in a Tea Shop

Cedar Hill Lions

Book 1: Lawman Lion

Book 2: Guardian Lion

Book 3: Rancher Lion

Book 4: Second Chance Lion

Book 5: Protector Lion

Christmas Valley Shifters

Book 1: The Christmas Dragon's Mate

Book 2: The Christmas Dragon's Heart

Book 3: The Christmas Dragon's Love

Elemental Mates

Book One: Mated to the Storm Dragon

Book Two: Mated to the Earth Dragon

Book Three: Mated to the Ocean Dragon

Book Four: Mated to the Fire Dragon

Book Five: Mated to the Griffin

Enforcer Bears

Book 1: Bear Cop

Book 2: Hunter Bear

Book 3: Wedding Bear

Book 4: Fighter Bear

Book 5: Bear Guard

Fire & Rescue Shifters

Book 1: Firefighter Dragon

Book 2: Firefighter Pegasus

Book 3: Firefighter Griffin

Book 4: Firefighter Sea Dragon

Book 5: The Master Shark's Mate

Book 6: Firefighter Unicorn

Book 7: Firefighter Phoenix

Fire & Rescue Shifters: Wildfire Crew

Book 1: Wildfire Griffin

Book 2: Wildfire Unicorn

Glacier Leopards

Book 1: The Snow Leopard's Mate

Book 2: The Snow Leopard's Baby
Book 3: The Snow Leopard's Home
Book 4: The Snow Leopard's Heart
Book 5: The Snow Leopard's Pack
Book 6: A Snow Leopards' Christmas

Gray's Hollow Dragon Shifters

Book 1: The Billionaire Dragon Shifter's Mate
Book 2: Beauty and the Billionaire Dragon Shifter
Book 3: The Billionaire Dragon Shifter's Christmas
Book 4: Choosing the Billionaire Dragon Shifters
Book 5: The Billionaire Dragon Shifter's Baby
Book 6: The Billionaire Dragon Shifter Meets His Match

Green Valley Shifters

Book 1: Dancing Bearfoot
Book 2: The Tiger Next Door
Book 3: Dandelion Season

Hideaway Cove

Book 1: The Griffin's Mate
Book 2: The Sea Wolf's Mate
Book 3: The Lightning Dragon's Mate

Hollywood Shifters

Book 1: Hollywood Bear
Book 2: Hollywood Dragon
Book 3: Hollywood Tiger
Book 4: A Hollywood Shifters' Christmas

Honey for the Billionbear

Book 1: *Honey for the Billionbear*

Book 2: *Guarding His Honey*
Book 3: *The Bear and His Honey*

Protection, Inc.
Book 1: Bodyguard Bear
Book 2: Defender Dragon
Book 3: Protector Panther
Book 4: Warrior Wolf
Book 5: Leader Lion
Book 6: Soldier Snow Leopard
Book 7: Top Gun Tiger

Lost Dragons
Book 1: A Mate for the Dragon
Book 2: Fated for the Dragon
Book 3: Destined for the Dragon
Book 4: A Bride for the Dragon

Ranch Romeos
Book 1: *Bear West*
Book 2: *The Billionaire Wolf Needs a Wife*

Rowland Lions
Book 1: *Lion's Hunt*
Book 2: *Lion's Mate*

Shifter Kingdom
Book 1: *Royal Guard Lion*
Book 2: *Royal Guard Tiger*

Shifter Suspense
Book 1: *Panther's Promise*
Book 2: *Saved by the Billionaire Lion Shifter*

Book 3: *Stealing the Snow Leopard's Heart*

Shifting Sands Resort
Book 1: *Tropical Tiger Spy*
Book 2: *Tropical Wounded Wolf*
Book 3: *Tropical Bartender Bear*
Book 4: *Tropical Lynx's Lover*
Book 5: *Tropical Dragon Diver*
Book 6: *Tropical Panther's Penance*
Book 7: *Tropical Christmas Stag*
Book 8: *Tropical Leopard's Longing*

Upson Downs
Book 1: Target: Billionbear
Book 2: A Werewolf's Valentine

US Marshal Shifters
Book 1: The Dragon Marshal's Treasure
Book 2: The Pegasus Marshal's Mate

Veteran Shifters
Book 1: Snow Leopard's Lady
Book 2: Lion's Lynx
Book 3: Panther's Passion
Book 4: Tiger's Triumph
Book 5: Jaguar's Joy

NON-SERIES BOOKS

Bears

A Pair of Bears

Alpha Bear Detective

Bear Down

Bear Mechanic

Bear Watching

Bear With Me

Bearing Your Soul

Bearly There

Bought by the Billionbear

Country Star Bear

Hero Bear

In the Billionbear's Den

Kodiak Moment

Private Eye Bear's Mate

The Bear Comes Home For Christmas

The Bear With No Name

The Bear's Christmas Bride

The Billionbear's Bride

The Easter Bunny's Bear

The Hawk and Her LumBEARjack

Big Cats

Alpha Lion

Joining the Jaguar

Loved by the Lion

Pursued by the Puma

Rescued by the Jaguar

Royal Guard Lion
The Billionaire Jaguar's Curvy Journalist
The Jaguar's Beach Bride
The Saber Tooth Tiger's Mate
Trusting the Tiger

Dragons
Silver Dragon
The Dragon Billionaire's Secret Mate
The Mountain Dragon's Curvy Mate
The Red Dragon's Baby

Eagles
Wild Flight

Griffins
Ranger Griffin
A Griffin for Christmas

Wolves
Alpha on the Run
Healing Her Wolf
Undercover Alpha
Wolf Home

SHORT STORIES IN ANTHOLOGIES

The Dragon's Choice, in Two Mates for the Dragon

CPSIA information can be obtained
at www.ICGtesting.com
Printed in the USA
LVHW090511190419
614798LV00001B/75/P